McCarthy's
Cave

Jack Doyle

iUniverse, Inc.
Bloomington

McCarthy's Cave

This is a work of fiction. All of the characters, names, incidents, organizations, and dialogue in this novel are either the products of the author's imagination or are used fictitiously.

iUniverse books may be ordered through booksellers or by contacting:

iUniverse
1663 Liberty Drive
Bloomington, IN 47403
www.iuniverse.com
1-800-Authors (1-800-288-4677)

ISBN: 978-1-4697-8578-3 (sc)
ISBN: 978-1-4697-8579-0 (hc)
ISBN: 978-1-4697-8580-6 (e)

Printed in the United States of America

iUniverse rev. date: 5/25/2012

McCarthy's Cave

Chapter One

A s I looked back later, it seemed that much of my life had been spent preparing for the series of events that began that spring, particularly my advertising career, and the hitch I did in the Navy Special Forces.

It really started that morning when Jennie, my secretary, assistant, confidant and love of my life, walked into my office at about nine-thirty. She laid a handful of envelopes on my desk.

"Here's the mail, Brian. Not too much, except some bills," she said, "although this one looks kind of interesting." She held up one of the envelopes and waved it at me. "Do you know any lawyers in Cave Junction, Kentucky?"

I frowned. "Cave Junction?" Then it came to me. "Well, I've got a cousin who lives down there, Joe Thomas, but he's a farmer, not a lawyer. Let's see it."

The return address on the envelope was Merton Caldwell, Attorney-at-law, 21 Main Street, Cave Junction, Kentucky. I opened it up and started reading it to myself. Jennie was standing there, tapping her foot, waiting, and I wondered how long it would take.

"If it's another one of your paternity suits I don't want to know about it"," she finally said.

"What do you mean, another one," I said, glancing up at her. "God, you're nosy for a secretary"

She turned around and headed for the door. "O.K., hot shot. Try sleeping on the couch tonight."

I laughed. "Come back here and sit down. I'll read it to you." Her curiosity was too much for her, as I had expected, so she came back, thumbed her nose at me, and sat down in one of the two chairs facing my desk.

"Dear Mr. McCarthy," I read." I am sorry to have to inform you that your cousin, Mr. Joseph Grady Thomas, passed away on February 11th of this year."

"We are in the process of settling his estate, which stipulates that all of his worldly possessions go to his nearest living relative. Our search has determined that you are that person, his wife Millie having passed away two years ago. They had no children. Please contact me at your earliest convenience so this matter can be properly settled, Sincerely, Merton Caldwell." It was signed in a large, scrawling handwriting.

"Well, well, well. Congratulations, Brian, you've come into an inheritance," Jennie said. "I kept hoping that someday you'd be worth something, although it was beginning to look a little grim. I guess it was worth the wait after all."

"Hey, sweetheart, if I ever get in the big bucks, the first thing I'll do is get myself one of those cute little twenty year olds, and bounce you right out of here on your ear."

Jennie laughed. "You couldn't handle it, hot shot. You'd better stick with someone who'll put up with your frailties."

"Well, I don't want to disappoint you and your dreams of riches, love, but I don't think we're going to become wealthy on the Joe Thomas estate."

"Darn it!" she said, snapping her fingers. "Who did you say this man was?"

"Joe Thomas was a cousin of mine. I spent a couple of summers on his farm when I was a kid. Let's see," I said, thinking back. "I was thirteen the second summer, so that was just about twenty-five years ago, and actually was the last time I saw him. As I remember Joe, he was a nice guy. Quiet, but friendly."

"Sort of like you."

I grinned, "Yeah, right. But that was a tough life trying to make a living down there. It's not exactly the best farmland in Kentucky."

"What were you doing down there?"

"Nothing much, really. I just went down both years for the summer. I worked a little for Joe, and played around, hunting, fishing on the little pond they had."

I smiled as I thought back on that summer "Yeah, I remember one night Joe took me out frog gigging."

"Come on, Brian. Frog gigging?"

I shrugged, "Hey, you California types don't know everything. Anyway, we went out in a little rowboat on his pond, after it got dark. The idea is that you shine the flashlight at the frogs, sitting on the bank, and it sort of hypnotizes them. Then you stick them with the gig, kind of like a long fork, and put them in a burlap bag."

"God, you must have been scared to death."

I ignored the sarcasm. "The fun part was when we got back to the farmhouse. Joe's wife, Millie, was in the kitchen, and when we came in she asked Joe if we had caught any frogs. He said "you bet", and dumped the frogs out on the floor. I didn't realize it until then, but they were still alive. God! The damn things started hopping all over the place. Millie screamed and ran out of the room, and Joe was laughing so hard he had to plop down on one of the kitchen chairs."

Jennie was laughing with me. "You're kidding!"

"Yeah. Then Joe told me to catch them and put them back in the bag. I couldn't say no in front of Joe, but I wasn't exactly crazy about the idea."

She got up. "Well, as fascinating as it has been, hearing about your amazing boyhood adventures, I'd better get back to work."

"It's about time," I said, and handed her the lawyer's letter. "See if you can get him on the line for me, would you?"

I watched Jennie as she walked out of the room, tall and willowy, really striking with that long brown hair swaying slightly. She's twenty-eight, but looks younger than that, and what a body. It was absolutely wonderful walking into a public place with Jennie, and watching all the guys follow her with their eyes. Great ego stuff!

My name is Brian McCarthy. Vital statistics, I'm thirty-eight years old, divorced, and no kids. I'm five feet eleven and a half, and when I was younger I always liked to round it off at six feet when somebody asked me, but the truth is I never quite made it. Not that it makes a hell of a lot of difference. Anyway, I'm at 185 pounds, a little heavier than I would really like to be, but that's a trade-off for a couple of beers every night, and I do work out two or three times a week. Not enough to get rid of the ten extra pounds, though. I still have a thick head of brown hair, and one of those square Irish faces, not good, not bad.

I spent four years in the Navy, right out of college, two of which were in a special forces kind of assignment. They taught me some nasty tricks, a few of which I still remember. One day I did some serious damage to my left arm, and that was the end of my Navy career, which was all right with me.

I own and run a small advertising and public relations business in Los Angeles, with the catchy name of McCarthy Communications, which I started ten years ago. Most of my clients are medium-sized industrial firms that don't have big ad budgets, so we've never been written up in Ad Age or any of the other advertising magazines. We're not viewed as a threat to J. Walter Thompson, and we're not going to be the next Jay Chiat or Hal Riney, but the business has been pretty good to me. It's provided me with a decent living, and a modest but nice two-bedroom house up in the hills near Universal Studios, which has appreciated in value a hell of a lot more than my advertising business.

We do all sorts of things for our clients, including trade brochures, price sheets, sort of a one-stop communications house for smaller businesses. I suppose the Harvard Business School would describe me as "moderately successful, but with a limited potential." They would be right.

Most of the bigger agencies are out on Wilshire Boulevard in the shiny new high rise office buildings, but I set up shop near the downtown area. Actually, the location is cheaper and it's also more convenient if you've got clients scattered around town, and when you're my size you take 'em anywhere you can get them. We've got seven employees, counting Bob Wagner who does most of our public relations stuff on a fee basis, and we're billing about two million dollars a year now.

Two million might sound like a lot of money, but that's what we bill, not what we make. We get fifteen percent of that in commissions, so we net about three hundred thousand, which covers our payroll and expenses. Plus we make some extra bucks here and there on collateral materials, which covers me, but there isn't a hell of lot left over at the end of the month.

Our billing has come down a bit over the past couple of years, and that's mostly my fault. The truth is that I've gotten sort of burned out on the whole thing, and haven't done a very good job of replacing the clients we've lost.

I must have been sort of day dreaming, and was startled when my phone buzzed. It was Jennie. "You taking a nap in there? Parker's coming in at ten," she said. Parker was the marketing guy for one of our better clients.

"Yeah, I know."

"And I've got Merton Caldwell on the line, Brian."

"Thank you, dear." I punched the button. "Mr. Caldwell?" The voice on the other end of the line was deep, formal, and with a slight Southern accent. He sounded older.

"This is Merton Caldwell."

"I'm Brian McCarthy, Mr. Caldwell. I received your letter this morning about Joe Thomas. I didn't know he had died."

"Yes, Mr. McCarthy. He passed away about a month ago. February the eleventh."

"I'm sorry to hear that. It's been years since I've seen him. How did it happen?"

"It was a heart attack, Mr. McCarthy, and apparently it was quite sudden. It happened out at the farm. The postman found him in the house, but by that time he was gone." I hadn't heard the expression postman in years.

"You mentioned that his wife Millie had also passed away."

"Yes. Millie passed away a few years ago. Joe lived alone."

"I see." I didn't quite know what to say.

There was one of those awkward pauses, and then he said, "You were not an easy man to locate, Mr. McCarthy."

"I suppose not, Mr. Caldwell. I don't have many ties back in that area any more, and I've been out here on the West Coast now for a number of years. Is there anything I need to do about this matter, or what would you suggest?"

"Well, there are papers to be signed, and some matters we really should discuss. All of that would be better if it could be done in person. Would it be possible for you to come back here? "

"Yes, I suppose I could. Let me take a look at my calendar. Just a moment." I put him on hold and studied my appointment book, and saw that the end of next week was clear.

"How would Friday of next week be for you, Mr. Caldwell?"

"That should be all right. About what time?"

"We'll probably fly into Louisville on Thursday, and drive down Friday morning. Say about one thirty?"

"Yes, that would be fine. Did you say we?"

I had figured on taking Jennie along, but didn't see any reason to explain that to Caldwell. "Yes, there will two of us.

"I see. Well, we'll plan on seeing you on Friday, then."

"See you then."

I hung up the phone and sat there, thinking about those times. I had things to do to get ready for my meeting with Parker, but my mind kept going back to those summers years ago, and what I remembered the best was the trip that Joe, Millie and I took to Mammoth Cave. That part of Kentucky is full of caves. The underlying rock formation is limestone in much of the area, and over thousands and thousands of years the water has eroded away the limestone, creating a whole system of caves, big ones, little ones, a lot of them interconnected if you found the right passageways.

The largest and most famous of them all, of course, is Mammoth Cave, and it was the first time I'd ever been in a cave anywhere.

The entrance to the cave starts as a big recess into the side of a hill. Then it narrows down into a small entrance, branching out from there into a labyrinth of narrow passageways connecting a series of rooms, some big, some small. Some of these rooms are filled with stalactites, the formations that hang down from the ceiling, and stalagmites, formations building up from the ground, caused by a slow, very slow dripping from the stalactites above them. In some places they finally meet, and merge together to form weird, flowing gigantic shapes in all sorts of colors. It is a magical, wonderful place.

I can remember the guide telling us that the temperature down in the cave was a constant fifty-four degrees, morning and night, summer and winter.

Some of the men who first explored these caves became legends, and the stories about them are told over and over again in that part of the country. Occasionally someone would get lost or trapped or would slip over the edge of a cliff, plunging to their death down in the darkness below. One of them, Floyd Collins, got trapped in a cave, and attracted huge national media coverage until he finally died down in there. He also had the dubious distinction of getting a cave named after him. When we first came back from the trip I would lay awake at night, thinking about those first explorers. What an adventure that must have been!

There's just something about caves that captures the imagination. When I was a boy I read "The Adventures of Tom Sawyer", and the scenes I remember best were the ones where he and Becky were lost in the cave, and were hiding from Injun Joe. That was scary!

The intercom buzzed, startling me out of my reverie. It was Jennie. "Parker's here."

"Tell him I'll be with him in just a second. I need to talk to you first."

She came in with a steno pad.

"How would you like to go back to Kentucky with me next weekend?" I asked.

She shrugged, "I don't know. I've never been there, but I've always wanted to go to the Derby."

"The Derby's not until May. Anyway, I've got to go down to Cave Junction and meet with this lawyer next Friday on this estate thing. Why don't you come with me?"

"Sure, why not." She was casual about it, but she would have been seriously pissed if I had gone without asking her.

"Book us into Louisville late Thursday on an open return. Also get us a rental car, and we'll drive down to Cave Junction Friday morning."

"O.K." She started to leave.

"Have you ever been in a cave, Jennie?"

She got this wicked grin on her face. "Why, Brian McCarthy. You wouldn't! Would you?"

It was kind of a thing between the two of us. We'd made love in some strange places. "Don't knock it until you try it, babe."

Just as she was leaving, Charlie the Dog, my pet, padded into the room, wagging his tail, demanding his morning walk.

"Do me a favor, will you?" I said to Jennie. "Take Charlie for his morning walk. Parker is here, and I've got a hunch this may get complicated."

Charlie who is part Dachshund and part Beagle showed up at our house about two years ago, looking beat up and hungry, so we adopted him. Jennie had moved in with me, and when we took him to the vet's, we were told that Charlie was about four years old.

We really didn't know anything about his background, but he had a collar on, so he must have belonged to some one. We had the feeling, from his behavior, that he had been out on the street for a while, and had had some rough times. He was a little grumpy with people at first, and especially with other dogs, but over time had gotten better. Anyway, he is our dog and we love him.

Parker worked for Branson Blades, a medium sized company that manufactured a line of tools. They were a steady if not spectacular advertiser, but they were growing, and I suspected, had some ambitious plans for the future, so they were important to us.

I went out to the lobby and got him. He seemed a little tense, which was not a good sign.

Chapter Two

We shook hands.

"How's everything with you, Les?"

"Could be worse. I guess. How about you?"

"Actually, things are going along pretty well. I suppose we could always use the General Motors account, but they haven't called. Anyway it's your meeting, Les. What's on the agenda?"

I would have put Les in his mid fifties, his hair turning grey around the fringes, about 20 pounds over weight, and basically a nice guy.

"Well, this is kind of tough, Brian, but we've been having some serious discussions recently, and the consensus is that maybe it's time for us to make a change."

Somehow I wasn't terribly surprised, but didn't want to show it.

"Wow. I'm surprised, Les. Shocked, really. We've been with you guys for several years now, and I thought things were going well. What's the problem?

"It's hard to pin it down, Brian. Maybe it's been too long, and perhaps its just time for a change."

"Can you be more specific?"

"I'm not sure I can, but we've been hearing good comments on some of the things our competitors are doing."

"Really? Why don't you bring some examples in and let us take a look? We review the competitive stuff constantly. Their ads are OK, but we haven't seen anything that we like better than what we're doing, Les. And believe me, we don't live in a vacuum. We try to stay very aware of what the other companies are doing. That's part of our job."

The discussion went on for a while. We finally agreed that we would have another meeting in a week or so, and look specifically at what they were talking about. My feeling was that our discussion ended on a somewhat more positive note than where it had started.

After he left I sat at my desk, thinking over the discussion we had just had. Bottom line, my feeling was that the account could be saved. Maybe. Losing it would be a real blow to the agency, and those kind of things get around the advertising community quickly, and could make other accounts nervous.

Jennie arrived back with Charlie in tow, and I filled her in on the meeting. Jennie and I talked about the business, almost on a daily basis, particularly about the accounts, and what our standing was with them.

She was surprised.

"As you know, Jennie, it's my account, one that I handle personally, so if there's a problem, I should have been aware of it."

"Don't beat yourself to death over it, Brian. Sometimes these things happen. We should find out more in the next meeting. You want me to pull all of the competitive stuff together?"

"Absolutely. We need to go over it very carefully. We don't need any more surprises."

"I'll have it ready by Monday. You want to schedule a meeting internally?"

"OK. How about 10 AM on Monday? Let's get you, me, Paul (*accounts*) Ron (*Finance*) and Dottie (*Creative*). I don't want to make our people nervous, but I am concerned about this."

The meeting went as planned on Monday, and I felt that we could make a good argument for our creative compared to anyone else. The question, of course, was whether or not the client would agree.

The following Thursday we flew into Louisville, picked up a rental car, a mid-sized Ford, and headed out for Cave Junction. There were no rooms available near the airport.

I have to tell you a little about Jennie, because she is absolutely the greatest thing that has ever happened to me.

It was just about three years ago that my secretary left to go off with some guy who was going on an expedition up the Amazon River, or some crazy thing. I never heard from her again, so I figured that maybe the piranhas ate her.

Anyway, I ran a help wanted ad in Ad Week for an assistant. I'd decided to upgrade the job, and really wanted someone who had some agency experience, and who could help me run the place.

Jennie Carson was the second person who responded to the ad. She was working for one of the big shops out on Wilshire, and, like a lot of us, loved the business but hated the big agency bullshit.

It's a funny thing. McCarthy's Law says that the bigger companies get, the worse they get. They become more political as they grow, and then you start getting all the back stabbing and character assassination. So you start your own shop, which of course will be a better place to work, especially if you own it. Naturally the objective is to build the business and make it grow to the point where it will be just as bad as the place you left, at least for the other people who work there. It's a vicious cycle.

Anyway, ten minutes into the interview I knew Jennie was the one I wanted. At the end of the interview I offered her the job at hundred bucks a month more than I had planned to, because I didn't want her to say no. Actually I was prepared to go higher, but she accepted, and I cancelled all the other interviews.

She started two weeks later, and was fantastic. I guess I just didn't realize how much help a really good assistant could be. She was bright, capable and generally great at handling situations. There were times when she could be a little caustic with people, especially "dummies" as she referred to them, but she was never that way with clients. She would have been great if she had been the ugliest broad in the world.

Not hardly. After the first few weeks she was there, I think we both knew it was only a matter of time before something happened. I was beginning to get to know the girl behind the protective shell, and was really curious to know why it was there. I suppose we were both fighting our impulses, trying to be professional or something. But first it was an occasional lunch, and then dinner, and then finally one night we ended up back at my place. We didn't waste much time once we got there.

God can she make love! Thinking back on my marriage to Lila, that whole relationship was all take and no give. As beautiful as Lila was, she was awful in the sack. It would probably be like living with one of those blow-up dolls they advertise in the skin books. After a while with Lila you thought, what's the point?

With Jennie the difference was night and day. She believed in sex, and thought the pill was the greatest invention in history. The first weird place we made love at was the Pomona Fairground. The occasion was the Los Angeles County Fair, and I'm told it's the largest county fair in the United States. Trivial Pursuit.

We had a client that was showing a new product at the Fair, a liquid fertilizer, which was typical of the kind of wildly exciting clients we had. We're talking really glamorous, exotic stuff. Yeah, sure. Jennie and I were just wandering around the Fairgrounds while the exhibits were being set up, looking things over, and we got to fooling around. I started out by patting her lovely little behind, then one thing led to another, and all of a sudden we were both in heat.

"Here?" she asked.

"Yeah," I said.

There weren't that many people around, and we found an empty john that had a couch in it. We locked the door and went at it like a couple of kids.

Jennie's a California girl, from an upper middle class family. Her folks live up in Santa Barbara now, and are nice enough, but I guess when Jennie was growing up, her parents had their own agenda, so she spent a lot of time by herself, or with baby sitters, to be more exact. On top of that she was an only child. Maybe that accounts for some of the shell, and the fact that she is a very independent person.

Anyway, Jennie went to UCLA, and she swims, surfs, skis, plays tennis and golf, and grew up leading that California lifestyle that all of us back East envied, whether we admitted it or not.

When we were running the hundred in eleven seconds, the California guys were at ten-five. When we were pole-vaulting eleven and a half feet, they were at thirteen feet. To us California was the "Golden Land", with a different breed of people.

After she was with me a few months, there was no doubt in my mind that Jennie and I would eventually get married. I didn't want her to get away. But we both had gone through bad marriages, and that makes you a little gun-shy.

I guess her marriage was a real bummer. We only talked about it once. It was one night after dinner, and we were sitting in the restaurant, just dawdling over a cup of coffee.

"You mentioned to me once that you had been married," I said. "Not too good, huh?"

She smiled, a sad, wistful kind of smile, and shrugged. "Yeah, not too good. Ted came from a lot of old Santa Barbara money. He was good looking, charming, and worthless as hell. Ted didn't need to work, and had no intention of doing so. Like a lot of people with too much time on their hands, he started drinking a lot, and was getting into drugs."

I nodded sympathetically. "I think I know the type."

"I really didn't know what to do about it, but we found ourselves squabbling and arguing all the time, and then he started staying out nights, and you don't have to be a genius to figure out how he was spending his time. There was no one I could talk to about it. My folks were always on the run somewhere, and his parents thought he had married beneath him anyway."

I just listened.

"Finally one night we really got into it, and he ended up hitting me a couple of times, and pretty hard. After he stormed out of the house, I packed up everything, and moved out. No son-of-a-bitch does that to me!" Her eyes flashed.

13

"Okay, okay. I hear you."

She smiled and put her hands over mine. "I'm sorry, Brian. I still get upset when I think about it. I guess that's why I don't think about it a lot."

"I understand, babe."

"Anyway, we were divorced. It was pretty easy, because I didn't want anything from him, much to his parent's relief, and about a year later he got pretty blitzed or stoned or something, up in the mountains at Lake Arrowhead, and went off the road coming back down. End of story. How about you?"

I shrugged. "That's probably enough pathos for one evening, but I'll tell you about it some time. It was pretty sordid."

We left early the next morning to catch a 7:30 flight to Louisville. We got in line to get our tickets, and I noticed a rather unusual man a couple of places behind us. He was wearing what appeared to be a rather expensive suit, which was all right, but it was not a great fit. He was about my height, but a little heavier, and had a thick head of curly black hair. I guess it was the hair that made him look unusual, at least to me.

I saw him again when he boarded our flight. Our eyes met just for a second, and then he looked quickly away. When we arrived in Louisville I saw him again, behind us in the car rental line.

The drive down to Cave Junction that Friday morning wasn't too cheerful. It was overcast and chilly, and although you could see a few buds beginning to pop out here and there on some of the trees, spring was late coming to Kentucky that year, and the landscape was still mostly stark and bare.

We stopped for a quick sandwich along the way, and had just sat down at a table, when my friend with all the curly hair came in. He sat at a stool along the counter without giving us a look.

"That's odd." I said.

"What?" Jennie replied.

"That man sitting there at the counter. I saw him at the airport this morning and then on our plane."

Jennie shrugged. "Maybe he's just interested in caves."

"Very funny."

We arrived in town at a few minutes before one. The sign at the edge of town said " Cave Junction, population 1349". The sign was rusted and looked like it had been there for a few years.

Main Street was in fact the "main street" of the town, and only ran for 3 blocks, so finding Merton Caldwell's office was not difficult, located in a two-story house, with a sign "Merton Caldwell, Attorney-at-Law" out in front. The sign looked like it had been there for a while also.

We went up on the porch and rang the bell. A minute or so later the door opened. An older man, tall and thin with a full head of gray hair, stood there. He looked at us, and said,

"Mr. McCarthy?"

"Yes. Mr. Caldwell, I presume?" After I said that I felt a little like Stanley, out in the African bush. I was a bit embarrassed.

"That's correct. Please come in."

"This is Jennie Carson, my fiance."

"Nice to meet you, ma'am."

We went into his office, which looked like it came right out of an old movie set, like Mr. Smith Goes to Washington or something. Merton Caldwell was sitting behind a massive mahogany desk, and the beautiful old wooden floor was partly covered by a faded green rug. An umbrella and overcoat were hanging from a coat tree in the corner of the room, and next to it was a huge roll top desk that you would kill for if you were into antiques. There were two large windows, one on a side wall and one behind him, and the view through them was distorted. The glass in them had obviously been there a long time, right out of the 1930's. There was only one item on his desk, a folder sitting right in the middle of it.

Caldwell was exactly what I had expected from the telephone voice, tall, about six foot two, thin, grey hair, black string tie, and very distinguished looking. He was probably in his early sixties, and you would instantly trust him with your life savings.

"I understand you're in the advertising business in Los Angeles. That must be pretty exciting," he said in that soft Southern drawl.

"Only when we have earthquakes," I replied. He didn't smile, so I decided I had better keep it serious. We sat down on a couple of straight-backed chairs with green velvet upholstered seats that sort of matched the rug, and which were getting a little frayed at the edges. "As you probably know, I grew up in Cincinnati, but I've been out on the West Coast now for about fifteen years, so I guess its kind of home."

"I've never been to California," Caldwell observed. "I keep telling myself I should go out there someday."

"Well, now that you know someone in California you should come out and visit." I was trying to warm things up.

He looked at me without blinking and said, "I reckon I know a few folks out there." The temperature didn't change. He glanced at his watch, reached for the folder on his desk, the sole item in sight, and took out a document, which he handed to me.

"This is your cousin's last will and testament."

Joe Thomas's estate was pretty uncomplicated. The items listed were the farm, the farmhouse, plus the furnishings and farm equipment. The farm was listed as one hundred and forty acres, with a loan still on it of about forty-six hundred dollars, payable to the First State Bank of Central Kentucky. Joe had evidently had to borrow some money during some bad times. There was no mortgage on the property, other than the loan I mentioned. When I had finished reading the will, Caldwell informed me that there was an insurance policy of two thousand dollars, and a bank account amounting to six hundred and twelve dollars, also with the First State Bank of Central Kentucky. I wondered why Joe kept the insurance policy after Millie died. Probably habit, or maybe just to cover his burial expenses.

I looked at Caldwell. "Is this my copy?"

He nodded. "Yes, you can keep that."

"Thank you."

"By the way," he said, "the estate still owes the Brockway Funeral Home six hundred dollars for Joe's funeral. I told them you were coming down and that I would mention it."

"Sure," I said, pulling a blank check out of my wallet. I always carried a couple with me, so I made out the check and handed it to him. He looked it over for a moment, and then opened one of his desk drawers, pulled out a piece of paper and handed it to me.

"While we're on the subject, here is the invoice for our legal services."

I looked it over quickly. Several items were listed, and the total at the bottom was seven hundred dollars. I was running out of blank checks, but when you're from the big city you have to act the part, so I wrote him out a check too. He seemed happier.

Caldwell reached in another desk drawer and pulled out a set of keys. "These are for the house. I suppose you want to go out and take a look."

"Yes, I'd like to. It's been a long time since I've seen the farm. It's hard to believe that it's been over twenty-five years."

He handed me the keys. "These are the papers for everything, the house, the barn, the tractor. "What do you plan to do with the farm, Mr. McCarthy? There could be some people around here that might be interested in buying it."

"I really don't know, Mr. Caldwell. This has all happened so fast. What is acreage going for in this area?"

"Last sale was about a year ago, the Bradley place, with a farm house about like yours sitting on it, went for something like $1200 an acre. Fella names Glenn Smith handles most of the real estate around Cave Junction."

"That's good to know. I appreciate that. Is the house OK to stay in?"

"Oh yes. It might be a bit cold but there's fire- wood on the porch and a fire place in the living room and in the main bedroom. The sheets have been changed. Here's a set of keys to get you in. Just as well. There are no Motels here in Cave Junction"

"Thank you for everything you've done." I took a card out of my wallet and placed it on the desk, taking one of his out of the card-holder on the desk. "Then I think we will be running along, Mr. Caldwell. We're going to be here for the weekend. Why don't we get together on Monday, say around ten o'clock?"

"Oh. A couple of other things, Mr. McCarthy." He took an envelope out of the folder and handed it to me. "your cousin left this out at the house. It's addressed to you. Also, the weather forecast says that there's a big storm coming in tonight. Very big, so be careful. That creek on your property's been known to overflow."

"Thank you. We'll see you Monday."

"I'll be here, Mr. McCarthy." He smiled politely, and we all shook hands again. I presumed there weren't too many appointments on his calendar. We had gotten directions to the farm from him, and Jennie and I headed out to inspect my inheritance.

I looked up at the sky. It was filling up with big, black ominous clouds. I pointed them out to Jennie. "It's looking a little nasty up there. They've been known to get some real gully washers around here."

"Gully washers?" she replied, with a quizzical look onn her face.

"Yeah. Gully washers. You know. Hard rain."

"That must a local expression. I'll try to remember that, Brian. Gully washers, eh?

We got in the car and after we drove a couple of blocks I pulled off to the side of the road and opened up the envelope my cousin had left for me. I could hardly wait to read it. All it contained was a handwritten note on plain white paper, a little aged, a little yellowed.

Chapter Three

Dear Brian,

My health is not doing so good, so I'm not sure how much longer I will be around.

Just a couple of things I wanted you to know since you are my only living close relative.

Firstly, I am leaving the farm and all the equipment on it to you. You can do whatever you want with this, but somehow I don't think you want to be a farmer. It's not an easy life but I never wanted to do anything else.

Secondly, a couple of years ago I discovered an entrance to a cave. I'm not a caver, so I talked Jim Adair, a friend of mine who is a caver, into going down into it.

He said that he discovered something strange down there, but he didn't want to talk much about it. You can contact him if you want, at 456-6169.

Love,

Joe

handed the letter to Jennie and started the car up again.

"It looks like you do have a cave down there." she said.

"Yeah, it looks that way, Jennie, but we'll just have to see what it's really like."

The Thomas farm was about eight miles east of town. The area began to look vaguely familiar as we drove along, and then I saw the house, sitting back from the road, about the same time that I saw the name Thomas, faded a bit, on the rusty mailbox.

The house was smaller than I remembered, but then your memory plays funny tricks on you. It was a boxy little place, white frame with green shutters. We turned off the main road and drove down the tree-lined lane to the house. As we drove up to the house it was obvious that it had been a while since it had been painted, and you could see where patches of paint were cracking and peeling away.

"Look, the swing's still there on the front porch. We used to sit out there in the evenings, waiting for it to cool off."

"Pretty wild," Jennie observed.

"Yeah, sometimes I'd catch lightning bugs and put them in a Mason jar."

"Lightning bugs?"

"Yeah, lightning bugs. I guess that's something else you California types still haven't seen. Maybe there will be some out tonight."

"What do you do with them."

"Do with them? Nothing. I'd just catch them and put them in the jar.

"With your bare hands?"

"They don't bite."

I took a practice swipe with my right hand.

"Like that," I said. "We'd punch some holes in the lid so they could breathe, and Millie would make me let them go before we went to bed."

"Yeah, I can see I've missed a lot. Wow!"

"Well, remember, this was before television, or at least before Joe and Millie had one. Of course you don't remember anything before TV."

"No. That's for you older folks."

Jennie and I went up the drive and I parked the car next to the house. The fields were sitting there untilled, and you could see patches of weeds springing up everywhere. By now Joe would have had the crops planted, stretching out in long, straight furrows, like the other farms we had passed on the way out, but there was no one to do it this year. On the other side of the drive was the creek. I walked over to the bank with Jennie. It wasn't much more than a trickle.

"You know, we had a hard rain toward the end of that summer I was here, and this creek went wild. It must have been four or five feet deep, just roaring through here." I pointed back along the creek away from the house. "There's a waterfall back there a little ways, maybe twenty feet high, and the force of the water that day carved out a pool at the base of the falls. All of a sudden I had my own private swimming hole, but by the end of the summer it had pretty well filled back up with rocks and silt. Let's take a look in the house."

I unlocked the front door to the house, and we went in. It was kind of an odd feeling going back into that place after all those years, and with Joe and Millie gone.

We walked through the house, which didn't take long. There were only five rooms, a living room, a small dining room, actually all the rooms were small, a kitchen and two bedrooms. It seemed to me that a lot of the furniture was the same stuff they had when I was there twenty-five years ago. There was a musty smell in the house, and I opened up some windows to get a little fresh air in the place.

Then I remembered that there was a cellar. I found the door to it out in the kitchen, turned on the light and went slowly down the steep, narrow stairway to the bottom, brushing away cobwebs as I went, and with Jennie right behind me. The low ceiling was about two inches above my head, and a single bulb illuminated the room. It was cold and clammy, as it was supposed to be, and as I looked around, there was nothing down there but a bunch of empty Mason jars lined up on the shelves.

"Look at all those empty jars," I said. "They used to put in a big garden in the summer. Grew all kinds of things, corn, beans, tomatoes, and then Millie would can the stuff for the winter. It looks like Joe just cleaned the jars as he used them up and put them back down here on the shelves, like Millie might came back some day and fill them back up again."

"Those last years must have been very lonely for him," Jennie said, her serious side showing. We went back upstairs, closed the door and sat down in the living room.

"Well, that's the tour, babe. What do you think?"

"It's perfect, Brian. Just what I've always dreamed about, becoming a farmers wife. You know, milking cows, shoveling manure, all that cool stuff."

I grinned. "Yeah, you'd be great at that, especially shoveling manure."

"I must say I don't care for all the cob webs in here, or spider webs, or whatever they are. How do you tell the difference?"

"I'm not really an expert on webs, but I guess if there's a spider in the web, it's a spider web."

"And if there's a cob in it, it's a cob web?"

"Very funny."

"What kind of spiders do they have around here?"

"I'm really not sure, Jennie. Probably black widows."

"Are they bad?"

"They're poisonous."

"You're kidding. Aren't you?"

"Well, if you'd like to get acquainted, there's one sitting on the couch next to you."

"My God." She jumped up, looking frantically around her.

I laughed. "Easy does it, babe. Just kidding. I'd better get a couple of fires started. There's some fire-wood out on the porch. We'll get them going and then go back in town and get something to eat at the Kentucky Colonel restaurant and diner.

"When do you think we can go back?" Jennie replied. You could tell that she was thrilled by this whole adventure.

"Probably Tuesday. I should go see Caldwell again on Monday before we leave." I went out in the kitchen and plugged in the stove and refrigerator, which both seemed to be still working. I had noticed an item on Caldwell's bill for electricity, so he had apparently kept the power on. "I suppose we ought to get some groceries," I said.

As the old saying goes, no one is perfect, and if Jennie had a flaw it would be her cooking. As a matter of fact, she could screw up ice water, and really didn't care. I cook a lot more than she does, mostly breakfast, and we usually eat our other meals out.

"I'll tell you what," I said. "Why don't we go over to see Mammoth Cave tomorrow. It's not all that far from here."

"I read somewhere that they have bats in caves." Jennie looked dubious.

"Not in Mammoth Cave. It's bat-less." I really didn't know. "Besides, they sleep most of the day."

"Sounds like my uncle Fred."

"Have you ever been in a big cave?" I asked.

"I've never even been in a little cave, Brian. Do you think we could make out?"

"Jennie, for Christ sake. You go through the cave with a guide and a bunch of other people."

She looked disappointed. "O.K. It was just a thought.

"Let's go get some lunch at the Old Kentucky Colonel restaurant. It's at least a five star."

"At least."

"Well, as I recall, it's also the only game in town. I'm kind of surprised it's still open. You know, we could probably buy the restaurant. Then you'd have something to do when you're not milking cows, or shoveling - you know -manure."

"Wonderful idea, Brian. Why didn't I think of that."

"Well, we might as well head for town"

When we walked out on the porch the first large rain drops started to fall. By the time we got to the restaurant, it was a downpour. There was only one other car in the parking lot, which had just pulled in behind us, and went all the way to the back. It was hard to see in the rain, but there was a man sitting in the front seat, who looked very much like my friend with the curly hair. This was no longer a coincidence. We were obviously being followed.

Jennie looked around the empty restaurant, then said "Do we have a reservation?"

"I hope so." We sat down at the counter and looked at the menu. The special was chicken fried steak.

"Jennie, have you ever had chicken fried steak?"

"Don't think so, but I've had chicken fried chicken."

"Try it, you'll like it."

Actually it wasn't bad. We finished dinner and started for home. The other car in the parking lot followed us onto the highway, keeping behind us at a reasonable distance.

When we got back to the farm, it was still early afternoon, and it had stopped raining. Jennie and I walked around the grounds for a little while, just looking things over, and letting the memories come slowly back from twenty-five years ago, and then we wandered back to where the waterfall had been. It was still there, but it wasn't quite as high as I remembered, like the house hadn't been as big as I remembered.

There was a barn out in back of the house, and I found a key that worked on the padlock. Most of the equipment in there was pretty old and rusty, except for a fairly new tractor, which probably explained why Joe had taken out the loan on the farm. When I looked up, I could see hundreds of tiny holes in the decaying roof, like stars twinkling in the sky at night.

It started raining again that evening, and kept on raining all day Saturday, so we decided that it was just too rotten out to try to drive over to Mammoth Cave. It had turned into a real, old-fashioned storm, with rolls of thunder that shook the house, and jagged arrows of lightning that briefly lit up the darkness, and at times you could hear the wind roaring through the trees. It would let up a little every once in a while, and then would come down again in a torrential downpour. As Billy Joe Pickens, one of my Texas buddies in the Navy used to say, like a "cow pissin' on a flat rock." Yeah, some Texans actually talk like that. As a matter of fact, Billy Joe talked like that all the time.

I had to look around the house to find coats and umbrellas so we could get out to eat on Sunday. Californians don't believe it ever rains or snows anywhere, so we never bother with incidental things like coats or umbrellas. I've gone to New York in the middle of the winter and forgotten to take an overcoat.

It turned cold on Saturday night, but there was a stack of firewood out on the porch, so I put a couple of more logs on the fire.

For a while we just sat on the couch together, watching the flames dance behind the fire screen, occasionally throwing another log on, comfortable in the silence.

Finally we settled down in the guest bedroom, still feeling like intruders in the house, which is probably why we didn't make love. We just cuddled up together, listening to the rain on the roof until we drifted off to sleep. Rain-drops on a roof are a pleasant sound at first, but after twenty-four hours it begins to get on your nerves.

It kept on raining on Sunday. On top of that, Jennie came down with a cold, and if there's one thing that makes her bitchy, it's being sick. She's one of those people that usually take a couple of weeks to get over a cold, and this one was starting out like it would be a classic; sneezing, runny nose, and she was starting to get a sore throat.

We sat in front of the fire reading, listening to Jennie's sneezes against the constant backdrop of the rain. I went out for food, looking around for our friend, but he was nowhere in sight. I brought some sandwiches back from the diner, but Jennie was feeling worse and just nibbled at the food. I had found a drug store in town, and brought Jennie back some Kleenex. I put a sack next to her on the couch to throw them in when they were used.

When the rain would let up a little you could hear the sound of the creek. It was roaring along now after two days of solid rain. I went out once and looked at it during a lull in the storm. That friendly little trickle had grown into a full-blown monster, maybe six feet deep now, and rushing past the house at a tremendous velocity, churning and boiling, carrying along tree limbs and trunks and all sorts of debris. The water was almost up to the bank now, and you wouldn't have lasted in that creek for five minutes.

The rain finally stopped during the night on Sunday, and Monday morning the sun came out. It was nice to see it again. The creek was still roaring, but it looked like it had gone down a foot or so already.

I wanted to see how my waterfall was doing after all that rain, so I picked my way carefully along the bank. The water was still high enough and swift enough to be dangerous.

When I got back there, just as I had thought it might, the pool underneath the falls had re-appeared. This time it was about twenty feet long and I guessed at least six feet deep at the base of the falls.

I stood there, taking it all in, when I noticed that a big hunk of the bank had caved in, just to the right of the falls, apparently washed away by the high water, and it looked like there was an opening of some sort.

It was tricky footing getting back there, but I made my way slowly along the edge of the creek until I reached a flat spot just in front of the opening. You couldn't see very far in, but it looked like the beginning of a passageway of some kind. It took a minute for it to hit me. "How about that! McCarthy, I'll bet that's the entrance to the cave that Joe mentioned in his letter.

I hurried back to the house as fast as I could to tell Jennie about my discovery. I was also a little nervous about leaving her alone.

As I might have suspected she was somewhat dubious about my discovery.

"You be careful, Brian. And you shouldn't be going in any old cave by yourself. You hear me?"

"Yeah, yeah. I hear you, but I know what I'm doing."

I didn't get an answer to that.

Chapter Four

I woke up early the next morning, and the first thing that popped into my head was the cave I had discovered yesterday.

Of course, without any light at the time, I could only see back into it a couple of feet, so I didn't really know anything about it, how big it was, how long it was, whatever. I knew I couldn't stand the curiosity, and really needed to take another look.

I had a flashlight out in the car that I could take along. I didn't want to wake up Jennie, especially with the cold she had caught, so I slipped on my clothes and shoes as quietly as I could.

I knew I probably shouldn't be going in the cave by myself, so I found a piece of paper, and wrote Jennie a short note, telling her where I was going, what time I left, 6:20, and that I should be back in an hour or so, most likely before she woke up. I put it on the couch where she would see it.

I eased out the door, got the flashlight out of the trunk of my car, and checked it out. It was working OK. Then I gently closed the trunk lid, and started back up the creek.

The water was down a foot or two, but it was still roaring along pretty good, and I still wouldn't want to end up in it. I didn't imagine that the creek originated in a large drainage area, so it would probably slow down pretty quickly once the rain stopped.

I peered into the cave entrance. The ceiling was about six feet high, just over my head. The floor was pretty level, and the cave itself appeared to head straight back into the hillside, at least as far as I could see from the entrance, and really did appear to be a cave of some sort.

I took a few tentative steps into the cave, pointing the flashlight ahead of me, moving slowly, frankly a little nervous.

After a few more feet I saw a small pile of rocks on the floor, with an opening above them. I pointed the flashlight up into the opening, which seemed to go back several feet into the ceiling of the cave. From what I could see, there appeared to be a lot of loose rocks still up in there. While I stood there, a few more rocks dropped down, next to where I was standing. I got the feeling that the whole mess up in there was sort of unstable.

Trying to step over the small pile of rocks, I tripped and had to grab onto the opening above me to steady myself. I guess that was all it needed, and now the rocks started pouring down. I quickly moved further into the cave to avoid them, and watched helplessly as they cascaded down, piling up in the cave right to the ceiling. I was trapped.

Fortunately I had the flashlight with me, and I had left the note for Jennie, so she would know where to come looking for me. I turned off the flashlight to conserve the batteries, which made it pitch black. There was nothing I could do but sit down and wait for Jennie.

It was deathly quiet in there for a while, but then I heard a scratching sound nearby. I turned the flashlight back on, and saw two large rats, just a few feet away, their beady red eyes staring at me. I hate rats!

I picked up a rock and threw it at them, and they turned around and ran. I turned off the light and waited in the dark. A few minutes later I heard that scratching sound again. This time when I turned on the light, there were four of them. The group was getting bigger. I threw another rock at them, hitting one. They disappeared again, but I had a feeling they would be back.

I sat in the dark, thinking about my predicament for a while, then turned on the flashlight and pointed it up at the ceiling. Then I stood up and began slowly pulling rocks away up at the top.

Most of the time, when I pulled a rock out, another one would slide down to take it's place, but occasionally they would hold, and after a while I was able to create a small opening. At least I would be able to communicate with Jennie when she showed up. Then I noticed that my flashlight was getting dimmer. I needed to conserve it, especially for the rats. I was sure that they would be back, so I turned it off and sat back down, glancing at my watch first.

It was 9:15. I had been in the cave for about three hours. Jennie should be along soon. I wondered what she was doing.

***

When Jennie woke up that morning she went out to the living room, looking around for Brian, and saw the note he had left for her.

"Brian, you idiot! What have you done?" She glanced at her watch. It was 8:30. He should have been back by now.

She quickly got dressed and started picking her way carefully along the bank next to the creek. Then a rock she had stepped on slid away in the wet mud, and her foot crashed down. She felt a sharp pain in her ankle, and fell to the ground. When she tried to get up, the ankle would just barely support her.

"Oh my God. I can hardly walk. I've got to get help for Brian. I know something has happened to him!"

She picked up a small tree limb, and using that for a crutch, managed to hobble back to the house.

She looked around frantically for the car keys, but couldn't find them.

"He must have taken them with him."

She picked up the limb, and slowly made her way out to the road.

"Some one's got to come along sooner or later."

Finally she saw a car approaching. She stood on the edge of the road, frantically waving as it approached, slowed down and then stopped.

An older man was driving it, and he rolled down his window.

"Is there some problem, ma'am?"

She explained her predicament to him, and then asked, "Do you know where Mr. Caldwell's office is?"

"Mr. Caldwell the lawyer?"

"Yes."

"Yes I do."

"Can you take me there? He's the only person I know around here."

"Yes ma'am."

They were back there in a few minutes, and he helped her up on the porch. They rang the bell and Mr. Caldwell appeared shortly.

"Hello Harvey. Hi Jennie. What are you doing here? Where's Brian?"

"I believe he's stuck in a cave. I need help."

"What do you mean?"

"I think he went back to explore that cave."

"By himself?"

"I think so."

"You never go into a cave by yourself. We had better get ahold of Adair. He knows as much about caves as anyone I know. Come in."

Harvey hesitated. "I'd better be running along. I've got some things to do."

Jennie smiled at him. "Thank you for your help."

"It's all right ma'am."

Caldwell was on the phone, having a serious conversation with someone.

"Well, Jennie, I just talked to Jim Adair. He knows as much about cavin' as anyone in these parts. He's got to get some equipment together and he'll be over. Shouldn't take too long. Then we'll take you back to the house."

"Can't I come along?"

"No ma'm. Not with that foot. I'm sure everything will be all right."

About a half hour later, two men showed up.

"Jennie, this is Jim Adair." He was middle-aged, short hair, slightly built but muscular.

"Pleased to meet you, ma'm. This is Will Johnson. We work together sometimes. We'd better get goin'."

A short time later Jim and Will arrived at the entrance to the cave. Jim looked at the area outside it carefully and then proceeded inside. It took just a moment to arrive at the pile of rocks.

"Hello," Jim yelled.

Brian had dozed off on the other side. The voice woke him up.

"Hello," he answered.

"This is Jim Adair. I'm here to get you out."

"Great! What do you want me to do?"

"Right now, just step away from the rocks. Can you do that?"

"OK."

Jim had a pick he'd brought with him. He buried the end of it in the rocks up at the top and tugged it toward him. A section of the rocks slid toward him. He continued doing this until he had opened up a hole a couple of feet wide.

"All right. I think you can climb out of there now, but be careful and move slowly."

Brian could see daylight at the top of the slide now. He moved carefully up to the opening, then crawled thru it and slid down the other side.

He stood up and shook hands with Jim Adair. "I'm sure glad to see you! I really appreciate your help. Is Jennie out there?"

"No. She sprained her ankle and is back at the house, but she's all right. I take it you went in this cave by yourself?"

"Well, I didn't go into to explore. Just to find out if it was really a cave."

"You're a damned fool, Mr. McCarthy. The first rule of cavin' is that you never go in a cave by yourself. Never!"

"I understand, Mr. Adair, and I was only going in a few feet."

"Looks like a few feet was enough to get yourself into a fix, don't it."

"I guess so, and I'm sorry I caused all this trouble. However, I would like to talk to you about helping me explore it. I understand you've been in this cave. As you say, Mr. Adair, I can't do it by myself."

"We'll talk about it, Mr. McCarthy. For now, let's just get back out of here."

Chapter Five

I bundled Jennie up that evening, just to get her out of the house for a while, and we went back to the diner again, which by this time was starting to get a little old. Jennie wasn't hungry anyway, but her ankle was a lot better.

"I think we're going to have to look around for another restaurant," I said after we had finished eating. "I've just set a new personal record for chicken-fried steak."

Jennie grinned. "That's down home cookin', son, and don't you forget it. It's what made America great," she drawled. "Seriously, Brian, when do you think we'll go back to L. A.?"

"I don't know, Jennie. It depends a lot on what we find in the cave this week. If it's a real cave, I'll have to decide what to do with it and with the farm property as well. In any event we'll probably go home in a day or two, and if I have to come back later I can come back here by myself."

The next afternoon we drove over to Adair's. Jennie was feeling crummy, and her throat didn't seem to be getting any better, but she insisted on coming along. As we came up the drive, Adair came around from the back of the house, another man walking with him.

We got out, and I introduced Jennie to him. Adair nodded. "This is Will Johnson, and he's gonna be going down with us, if we go. We've worked together before." We shook hands all around.

Johnson was about the same age and the same slender, wiry build as Adair. In fact, they almost looked like brothers. The thought occurred to me that going down into caves was probably easier for smaller guys.

"My cousin Joe left me a note with the lawyer. It said that you'd been down in the cave."

"That's true." Jim said. "Will and me, that is. I wouldn't go in there by myself."

"He said you found something strange in the cave?"

"That's true."

Brian looked directly at him. "And you didn't want to talk about it?"

"Well, I wouldn't exactly say that. Whatever it was, I had never seen it before, didn't know what it was, so there wasn't much use in talking about it."

"Can you take me to it?"

Adair shrugged, "I reckon so. I don't think it's very far once we get in there."

"I want to go."

"Did you get the clothes I mentioned?" Adair asked.

I had picked up some things at a local store, took a sack out of the car and handed it to him. "These O.K.?"

He looked through them, nodded and handed them back to me. "Let's go around back and I'll show you the equipment." We walked around to the back of the house where a number of items were laid out on a table.

"Let's start with this. It's probably the most important thing we'll talk about." He picked up a miner's hat, with a lamp securely attached to the front of it.

"This is your carbide lamp, " Adair said. "You've got to have light down there, and this will run for hours. We've got some candles and flashlights in case of an emergency, but neither one will last very long."

"O.K.," I nodded, paying close attention to what he was telling me, and remembering what had happened to my flashlight when I was digging my way out of the cave.

"I'll show you how it works. You put these lumps of carbide here in the bottom of this jar, and water in the top." He pointed to the jar on the front of the miner's hat. Both items were already in there. "When I turn this here valve on top, the water will slowly drip down onto the carbide, making acetylene gas, which is forced out here. See that?"

"Right," I said.

He pointed at a spot in the middle of the reflector, mounted on top of the jar. He cupped his hand over the reflector to trap some of the gas, and hit a small, serrated wheel at the top of the reflector, which grated against a flint, causing hot sparks. The gas ignited with a pop and the torch was on.

"Pretty slick," I said.

"They's more water and carbide in these plastic bottles," Adair said. Then he picked up an empty plastic bag that was lying on the table. "After the carbide is used up, we put what's left of it in this bag and bring it back out and bury it. It's nasty stuff to leave lying around. Now you try it."

He handed me another lamp with nothing in it, and a couple of bottles. I took some carbide lumps out of one bottle and put them in the bottom of the lamp, and then poured some water from the other bottle into the top.

Adair nodded. "All right. You're doin' fine."

I opened the valve and watched the water slowly start to drip on the carbide. It took a couple of tries with the spark lighter, which was really sort of like the flint apparatus on a cigarette lighter, and the lamp ignited.

"That's good. Now try it again," Adair said.

He watched while I lit the lamp two more times, apparently satisfied now that I knew how it worked. I appreciated his thoroughness.

There were three small back packs on the table. "Everything will go in here," he said. He began to point out the other items on the table. "These are spare parts for the lamps, gaskets, burner tips and tip cleaner. There are matches in this water-tight container, some canned food, candy bars, a jack knife, a pair of pliers, and a can opener." He paused. "There's rope if we need it, candles, flashlights and a first-aid kit. Also they'll be fresh water in these canteens."

"Do you want me to take some of these things back in my car?" I asked.

He shook his head. "I'll pack it all and bring 'em over in the morning. We'll be over at your place at seven-thirty."

"I'll be ready."

Jennie finally spoke up, her voice kind of croaking. "Mr. Adair, I want to go along."

"Well, ma'am, I'm afraid we can't do that." He nodded at me. "We've got one tenderfoot along as it is, and that's enough. Besides, we need someone on the outside. We're goin' in there at eight o'clock tomorrow morning, and we're plannin' on comin' out around four o'clock tomorrow afternoon. You give us two more hours. If we're not out of there by six, I'm going to give you a man's name to call, and you call him and tell him we may be in trouble. Understand?"

Jennie nodded meekly, which wasn't like her.

Adair smiled. "Besides that, you don't sound too good, ma'am. You wouldn't want to go down in a cave with that cold you got. But I'll tell you what. Once we know what's down there, providin' it's safe and there's somethin' down there worth seein', I'll take you down myself." That sort of surprised me, but then Jennie had that kind of effect on men.

The rest of the day dragged by, and I thought it would never end. We tried another restaurant over in Burtonville, and decided that our diner was better. We picked up a couple of books at a drug store and went back to the farm, but I had trouble concentrating on my reading. I finally went to bed at ten, setting the alarm for six, but it must have been a couple of more hours before I drifted off to sleep.

I awoke with a start when the alarm went off, disoriented like you get sometimes when you're sleeping in a strange place, and it took me a moment to figure out where I was. Jennie stayed in bed, sort of dozing, and I got up, shaved and took a bath. There was no shower in the house. I cooked some bacon and eggs for myself, since Jennie doesn't eat much for breakfast, but I took her in a hot cup of coffee.

I shook her gently. "Wake up, Jennie. Adair will be here pretty soon."

She looked up at me, and shook her head. "Are you really going down in that cave?"

"Looks that way, babe."

"You be careful."

Obviously no two people are alike, and I guess one of the differences between Jennie and me is that I tend to be more impulsive, to do things on the spur of the moment, whereas Jennie is more analytical. She usually thinks things over pretty carefully, at least important things. I have to admit that her approach has stopped me on occasion from doing some pretty silly things, but I didn't see anything silly about going down in the cave. That was something I had to do!

Promptly at seven-thirty I heard a car coming up our lane. I looked out the kitchen window, saw Adair and Will Johnson in Adair's Chevy pick-up truck and walked out to greet them.

Adair got out of the truck. "Good mornin'." He looked me over critically. I had put the overalls over the sweater, and had managed to get the boots on over two pair of socks. I figured that would keep my feet warm. I'd had to dress for lots colder weather in the Service than we would encounter down in the cave.

"Good morning, Mr. Adair. Mr. Johnson."

Adair grinned, "You sure you still want to do this, Mr. McCarthy?"

I grinned back. "I can hardly wait."

"Well then, let's go take a look."

He went to the back of the truck and handed me a back pack. "Let's get that on snug. We don't want to lose it." He watched, satisfied, as I put it on.

"Here's your hat and knee crawlers," He said. I put the knee crawlers on, as did Adair and Johnson. The hat had a strap and I adjusted it to fit fairly tightly.

"Where's the lady?" Adair asked.

"Jennie?" I called.

She came out.

"Mornin', ma'm," Adair nodded at her.

"Good morning, Mr. Adair."

He took a piece of paper out of his shirt pocket and handed it to her. "That's Sam Briscoe's name and phone number. Remember now. If we're not back out of the cave by six o'clock sharp, you call him. Don't wait."

I added, "The car keys are on the dresser in the bedroom, Jennie. The nearest phone is at the gas station just before you get into town."

She looked at both of us, and her eyes were a little moist. Maybe it was the cold. "I'll take care of it. You take care of Brian, Mr. Adair."

"Yes ma'm." He looked at me. "Well, let's go have a look at your cave, Mr. McCarthy."

I led the way back along the creek to the opening, Jennie following behind us.

Adair stood there for a minute looking at the opening. He stepped inside the entrance to the cave, looked quickly around and then came back out again. Then he stepped back and looked at the area above the cave entrance. It was a vertical cliff, going up about forty feet or so, mostly a bare outcropping of rock.

Finally he drawled, "You know, you just might just have something here, Mr. McCarthy."

"Really? How can you tell?"

"It just kinda looks like cave country," he said. "What do you think, Will?"

"Could be, Jim" Will said, delivering one of his extended speeches.

I was starting to get excited again. Adair quickly lit the lamp on his miner's hat and started into the cave. "You follow me, Mr. McCarthy, and Johnson'll bring up the rear. Right now we'll just light one lamp." I was surprised at how much light the lamp generated.

"Is that the rock fall you told me about?" he asked, stopping when we got to that point.

"That's it," I replied.

He shook his head. "I don't rightly care for the looks of that," he said. "We'd better open it up some more, Will, because we won't get through with them packs on anyway. You wait over there by the entrance, Mr. McCarthy."

The two of them worked away at it, slowly and carefully enlarging the opening another couple of feet. When he was satisfied with the size of the opening, he pointed the lamp up into the crevice, and studied that for a moment or so, then walked back to where we were standing.

"Let's hope that bugger don't cause no problems," he said, pointing up at the crevice. He turned and looked at Jennie, standing at the entrance. "Remember, six o'clock, ma'am." Then he turned back toward the cave. "Well, boys, I guess we might as well have a go at it."

I hadn't had these kinds of mixed emotions, both excitement and apprehension, since that night I lowered myself into those cold, dark waters, off of Los Angeles, heading for my first practice mission.

Chapter Six

Jim Adair led the way. He told me to stay two or three feet behind him, with Will Johnson about the same distance behind me, bringing up the rear. I guess the idea was that if they put the tenderfoot in the middle, between the two experienced guys, he would get in a little less trouble.

The first obstacle was the rock pile. With the clearance that Adair had made, scrambling over it was no problem now. We reached a turn in the passageway, and as the tunnel began turning to the right, the floor of the cave also started to slant slightly down. This was farther than I had gone in my brief excursion on Monday, so what lay ahead was new territory and I could feel my heart beating faster. I was a little surprised at just how excited I was.

Jim moved slowly ahead, shining the lamp at all angles of the cave, looking things over, taking his time. There was no doubt in my mind that I had found the right man. The professionalism, the attention to detail was obvious, and very reassuring. In a way, Jim Adair reminded me of the guy who gave me most of my combat training in the Navy, Vince Fernandez. They both had the same slow, careful, methodical approach to things, which might explain why Vince is still alive, growing avocados down in Fallbrook, California, and why a lot of us he trained made it back from the service with him. Vince is one of the guys I still stay in touch with, and I will be forever grateful to him.

We moved slowly down the passageway, which was getting smaller, becoming a little narrower and not quite as high. We were stooped way over now, and I kept bumping my head on the ceiling, glad that I had the miner's hat on for protection. I was beginning to appreciate what this caving was all about. It took a special kind of person to go down into a cave. There was a real sense of isolation in the close, cramped quarters, surrounded by utter silence and darkness. You felt constricted on all sides, like the cave was closing in on you. I could understand now what Jim Adair had meant when he had talked about people getting panicky down here. I found myself fighting that feeling, and I had never had a problem with claustrophobia.

Ahead, illuminated by Jim Adair's lamp, I could see that the tunnel made an abrupt turn to the right. We moved slowly ahead, picking our way over the rocks underfoot. When we made the turn we saw that the tunnel now divided in two. The left fork continued downward, while the right fork appeared to level out somewhat.

"Wait here," Adair said. He took the left fork and quickly disappeared from view.

"What's he doing?" I asked Will Johnson, not able to see him in the darkness that surrounded us.

"He's just figurin' out which way to go," Johnson said. "He won't go far by himself. You never do that down here."

He was right. A couple of minutes later we saw the light coming back and Adair re-appeared. Without a word to either one of us he started down the right fork and disappeared again. Johnson and I waited, and shortly he showed back up again.

"It's hard to tell," Adair said, "but if we want to keep goin' and find some big rooms, it looks to me like we ought to take the left fork. That one looks like its gonna head on down into the cave. The right fork seems to stay up higher. Course you never know what we'll find later on."

"You're the boss", I said. "You call it."

"We'll go left," he said without hesitation. He looked at me. I was squatted down now, tired of being stooped over by the low ceiling.

"How you gettin' along, Mr. McCarthy?" he asked.

"Just fine, Mr. Adair."

We started out again, still crouched over, moving slowly. Then we reached an area where the tunnel started getting bigger again. It was wider now, with a higher ceiling, and we were finally able to stand erect, which was really a relief. Then we hit a stretch where we were climbing over bigger rocks, and the path, or floor, or whatever it was called, was a lot more rugged.

Adair stopped and turned to us. "It looks like it's starting to drop off on the left there." He pointed. "Will, maybe you better light your lamp too."

We waited until Johnson's lamp was on, and then continued slowly. There was a drop off on the left, and it seemed to be getting deeper. Adair stopped to take a powerful flashlight out of his back pack, then every few feet after that he'd stop and direct the beam over the side. We had now reached a point where the light didn't reach the bottom. Every so often he'd find a small rock and toss it over the side, listening until it hit down below.

"Sounds like it's a hundred feet down, anyway," he said.

In places our pathway narrowed down to not much more than a narrow ledge, no more than a couple of feet wide, and in some spots the ground was damp, making it slippery going.

"Be careful, Mr. McCarthy," Adair said. "This is right dangerous through here."

I didn't answer, but pressed myself up against the wall on my right, edging myself along and watching carefully where I put my feet, moving one small step after another, well aware that if I slipped I'd go over the side into that deep, dark chasm below. The going was very slow, and it occurred to me, with some feeling of discomfort, that we would eventually have to re-trace every step we had taken. "Well, McCarthy," I said to myself, "you were the one that wanted to come down here."

Finally the path widened out again, and I let out an audible sigh. Adair must have heard it, and he looked at me with a slight grin on his face. The next time Adair threw a rock over the side we heard a splash down below. He listened intently for a minute, and then tossed another rock down. "Don't hear no water runnin', so it must be a lake, Will, but it sure sounds like a long way down there now," he said.

Will Johnson was a man of few words, and as usual did not reply, nor apparently did Adair expect him to.

The going was easier now, and we continued for some time, with the wall on our right, which seemed to go up some distance above us, and the chasm on our left.

The space on our left seemed to extend out quite a ways, and I had the feeling that if this whole area was illuminated so that we could see it, we'd find ourselves in a huge open space. We had continued to descend at a slight angle.

"How deep are we underground, Mr. Adair?" I asked.

He stopped walking. "Hard to say exactly, but I imagine a hundred feet anyway. Maybe deeper."

I glanced at my watch, surprised to see that it was almost eleven o'clock. I presumed that we wouldn't be able to go too much farther today if we were going to stop to eat, and get back to the entrance by four o'clock.

A few minutes later Adair stopped in front of me. "We may be coming to something, Mr. McCarthy," he said.

The wall had suddenly re-appeared on our left side and we were now entering what appeared to be, in the limited light we had, a large chamber. The floor was fairly level, but the ceiling vaulted away. Ahead I could see vague shapes and structures, outlined in Adair's lamp. "Light your lamp, Mr. McCarthy. I think you'll want to look around."

We waited while I got the lamp going, and then he turned on his powerful flashlight. As he swept it around the room I gasped, awed by what I saw. It was a fairyland! The room itself was large, perhaps sixty or seventy feet long, and almost the same width, and the ceiling was high, itself perhaps thirty or forty feet to the top. It was hard to tell the distances exactly in the dim light we had.

On the right side of the room was a massive, magnificent display of stalagmites and stalactites, meeting each other in huge columns, and in places forming a cascade of shapes and forms and colors. I stood and shook my head is disbelief, thinking of the thousands and thousands of years it had taken for all of this to take form. And we were perhaps the first human beings to ever see it. At least so far I hadn't seen any traces of anyone else. But then I hadn't really been looking.

"Tell me, Mr. Adair," I asked. "Do you think anyone else has ever been down here?"

"Well, ain't seen no signs of anybody, but it's possible. We weren't in this part of the cave. You seen anything, Will?"

"Nope," replied the loquacious Mr. Johnson.

Jim Adair walked over to one of the formations and ran his hand across it. "They's wet. Still formin'. That's quite a sight, Mr. McCarthy." What he was saying was that the cave was still forming, that the stalactites were still growing down from the ceiling, and with their slow, almost imperceptible process, were dripping down to form the stalagmites below them.

"Yeah." I remembered vaguely some of the rooms I had seen in Mammoth Cave, and wondered how this would compare. I would have to go back to Mammoth again just to see for myself, but no matter what the comparison was, good or bad, this room was different. It was mine!

As I walked toward the rear of the room, the formations became thinner, more delicate, and in places were still separated, tapering toward each other from both the ceiling and the floor. The back wall, like the left side, was solid rock, except for a small opening where the tunnel appeared to continue. Adair and Johnson examined the walls of the room carefully, shining the lamps into every nook and cranny. "Well," Adair said finally, "if she keeps on goin' I reckon it must be through there." He pointed at the small opening that I had seen. "We should probably stop n' eat now," he continued. "We can't go much further today, anyway. Got to start back around one o'clock."

When we finished eating we put everything carefully back in the packs, leaving nothing behind.

Adair looked at the tunnel and then his watch. "Well, we can go a little ways. but this is goin' to be a kinda tight, fellas. You may get a chance to use them knee crawlers yet, Mr. McCarthy."

He was right. After a few minutes we were down on our hands and knees. Our progress was getting slower and slower as Adair took a lot of time examining the tunnel walls. This would be no place to run into a rock slide. I shuddered at the thought. Finally the tunnel was so small that Adair stopped moving. He took out the flashlight, and pointed ahead down the tunnel. It continued to narrow, reaching a point where it would be impossible to move through.

"Well, Mr. McCarthy, it looks like that's about it, at least for this tunnel."

"Yeah, it does." I really felt closed in now, and didn't like it, but no way would I say a word about it to Adair.

"Will, back out until you can turn around, and let's go back to the room," Adair said.

When we got back there I spent a few more minutes looking around. "You think we'll be able to bring Jennie down here, Mr. Adair? I'd really like to have her see this."

"I reckon so, Mr. McCarthy. I don't think there's anything on the way down she can't handle, long as she don't mind bein' in some tight places. I'll have to put in a rope where that drop-off is."

We started back, still moving slowly, carefully, until we reached the place where the cave forked off in two directions.

"If you like, we'll try that left one tomorrow, Mr. McCarthy," Adair said. "I think we've had enough for one day. Tomorrow we'll go find that stuff I was telling you about."

"Yeah, I sure would like to look at the other tunnel, Mr. Adair. That room we found was great, but I was kind of disappointed when the tunnel ended back there. I was hoping it would keep on going."

"Well, you never know with caves. There might be some tunnels down there where we had the drop-off, but climbin' down in there with rope ladders is tough goin'. To be honest about it, Mr. McCarthy, I'm not sure I want to get all that involved."

I nodded. "Well, let's see what happens tomorrow when we try the other one."

We continued, quickly reaching the rock-slide area, and then we were out of the cave, back out in the sunlight. It was nice to see it again. It was just three-thirty, and we had been down in the cave for seven and a half hours. I felt absolutely drained.

As we got back near the house, I called out, "Jennie. We're back."

She came running out of the house and threw her arms around me. "Oh, Brian. I was so worried. Are you alright?"

I grinned at her. "You bet I am, babe. We found a great room down in the cave, and Mr. Adair says he can take you down there. I'll tell you all about it after we get these fellas on their way. What time tomorrow, Mr. Adair?"

"I reckon about the same time. We'll be out here about seven-thirty. You O. K. tomorrow, Will?"

Johnson nodded agreement. "Yep."

I shook his hand. "It was a great day, Mr. Adair. Thank you."

"Glad you enjoyed it, Mr. McCarthy." He smiled. "It was kind of fun for me to go down there."

"You want to leave the back packs here in the house?" I asked.

"No, I reckon I'll just take 'em along," he said. "See you in the morning. Night, ma'am."

After they left I popped open a cold beer, which after the day I had been through went down about as good as any beer I've ever had, and I poured a little Jack Daniels over ice for Jennie. "This will be good for your cold. How's it coming?"

She shrugged. "About the same. These damn colds always seem to take forever to go away." Her voice was still hoarse and raspy. "I'll be glad when we get back home, but I'm really glad you found something down there, Brian."

"Boy, I wish I'd had a Polaroid down there. I'll have to see if I can do that next time we go down."

We sat there sipping on the drinks and I told her about the events of the day, still excited about what we had found, and starting to relax. I looked out the window as the sun was starting to set. "Back to the diner?" I asked.

"Why don't you do ahead, Brian. I really feel lousy. Maybe you can bring me back a sandwich."

I felt sorry for Jennie, because I knew she felt rotten. I also knew that she wouldn't be able to go down in that cave with Jim Adair until her cold started to clear up, and that wouldn't be on this trip to Kentucky I was feeling the effects of the day by the time I got back from the diner, and I went to sleep about thirty seconds after I hit the mattress. I guess caving takes its toll. But my last thoughts before I drifted off to sleep were about the other tunnel we hadn't explored, and what we might find tomorrow.

Chapter Seven

The next morning Adair and Will Johnson showed up right on time at seven thirty. I had been up for an hour, shaved, bathed, had eaten my breakfast of bacon and eggs again, and could hardly wait to get back down in the cave.

"Good mornin', Mr. McCarthy. You ready to try this again?" Adair asked.

I smiled at him. "Ready to go, Mr. Adair. Although I sure did sleep real good last night." I was starting to talk like Adair. It was catching, like watching Gary Cooper or Jimmy Stewart in a western movie.

"Well, let's get at it," he replied. As usual, Will Johnson added little to the conversation. He was really a nice guy and pleasant to be around, just not what you'd call talkative.

I put the knee crawlers back on, fastened the back pack securely and then he handed me the miner's hat. I noticed that the knee crawlers had been washed, if they were the same ones, and the lamp on the hat had been cleaned out, but then I would have been surprised if those things hadn't been taken care of.

"Jennie, we're leaving," I called. She came out the door in her bathrobe, and put her arms around me. "You be careful, Brian." She turned to Adair. "You too, Mr. Adair." As she let go of me, her robe parted in front, revealing her for just a moment in a very sheer negligee, almost nude. I think Will Johnson showed more reaction to that than to anything since I'd met him. But then Jennie looks better just crawling out of bed in the morning, even with a cold, than most girls do when they're healthy and have been up for hours primping in front of a mirror. I'm sure Adair caught it too.

"Remember, Miss," Adair said. Jennie had suddenly switched from being "ma'am" to "miss", and I figured it must have been the negligee. "The instructions are the same as yesterday. We plan to be back out of there by four o'clock. If we don't show up by six, you call Sam Briscoe. You still got the number?" Always checking the details.

"Yes I do."

We started back to the cave in single file. When we got to the creek I looked back, and she was standing there, watching. We both waved.

"That sure seems like a mighty fine woman you got there, Mr. McCarthy," Adair said.

"Yeah, she's a brick," I said.

"A brick?"

"Yeah, I mean she's great."

"A brick," he mumbled to himself.

In a short time we were back at the two forks in the cave. As we started into the tunnel on the right, the path seemed to be more irregular and bumpy. As Adair had observed a couple of days ago, when you tour a maintained cave, like Mammoth, you don't realize that they can be different, and lot more rugged in their natural state.

"Better turn on your lamp, Will," Adair said." It's a little rough in here. We could use some extra light."

This passageway now started heading slightly down, which I found encouraging. I figured we had to get down deeper to find rooms like the one we had found yesterday. However, the bad news was that the ceiling was becoming lower, and we found ourselves crouching down more.

"Gettin' pretty narrow up ahead," Adair said. "Looks like we'll do a little more crawlin' today."

And we did. Shortly, we were back down on our hands and knees, creeping along the tunnel. No one would ever convince me that this was the fun part of caving, and I was starting to get that feeling again of everything closing in around me.

"You think we're running out of cave?" I asked.

"Hard to say. It might widen out again. We'll just keep goin', but it's going to get a little tight."

Yeah, tight. Now I could feel the back pack bump occasionally on the ceiling, and I was definitely starting to feel a little claustrophobic. We were moving very slowly now, and we couldn't have come all that far from the cave entrance. Adair continued to carefully check the sides and top of the tunnel as we progressed, making sure that nothing could come down to trap us.

The narrow section wasn't really all that long as it turned out, and the tunnel began to enlarge to the point where we were able to stand up again. He was a few feet ahead of me, as I was still moving out of the narrow part of the passageway.

"Looks like we got somethin' coming up here," Adair said.

I got up close behind him to look. We were coming into a room, but this one looked to be about half the size of the one we found yesterday. As it turned out, there wasn't a great deal to see. On the right wall there was a small series of stalactites and stalagmites, none of which had yet joined together. Following Adair's lead from yesterday, I touched a couple of them, and found them to be wet, so they were still in the formation process.

"Be careful what you touch, Mr. McCarthy. It can change things down here for a long time."

"Thank you. I'll be careful, Mr. Adair."

Over on the left wall there were some clusters of what looked like flower petals, curling away from the wall. Adair saw me looking at them and walked over.

"There used to be lots of them in some of the caves at one time, but years ago folks started chippin' 'em off the wall and would take 'em home. That was before they got the caves under control. Sure was a dumb thing to do. Now nobody can't see 'em, just sittin' at home in somebody's cigar box or got thrown out." He reflected for a minute. "When I was a kid I chipped off a few myself, so I reckon I'm as bad as the rest."

This room was obviously not as exciting as the one we found yesterday, but I was encouraged by the fact that at least we were finding something.

We left the room and continued on down the passageway. After a short distance two things began to happen, the passageway started getting narrower again, and it started slanting upward toward the surface. Not a good sign, I thought.

Pretty soon we were down on the ground crawling again, and I found myself disliking that claustrophobic feeling more and more. The thought was beginning to occur to me that maybe I wasn't cut out to be a caver or spelunker or whatever it's called after all, although I would hate to admit that to anyone, especially Adair. I had really gotten to like him. I just didn't want to give him the satisfaction of knowing that I was uncomfortable down there, but he probably knew it anyway.

Now the passageway started to enlarge again, and I saw Adair getting back up to his feet. I was three or four yards behind him, trying to catch up, when I heard him say "What the hell - - ?" His voice sounded strange.

"What's the matter?" I asked.

He moved to one side so I could see past him. I could see by his flashlight that we were coming into another room. I moved next to him as he aimed the beam all around the area. It was a small room again, about the size of the last one than we had found, maybe twenty-five or thirty feet long, about twenty feet wide, and only about eight feet or so high.

There was an eerie, pale color being reflected from the room, almost like the ceiling and walls were glowing in the beam of the flashlight.

"What in the world is that?" I asked.

"I dunno," Adair answered with a kind of wonder in his voice. "That's the stuff I was telling you about." Will Johnson came up behind us.

"My Lord," I heard him say.

"You ever seen anything like that before, Will?" Adair asked.

"Mercy, no, Jim, I never seen anythin' like that before in all my born days." It was the longest sentence I had heard Will Johnson speak.

The sight we were looking at was one of the strangest, weirdest things I've ever seen. The whole ceiling of the room was thickly covered with some kind of a pale, yellow-white vegetation, and it was growing half way down the walls as well. I walked up to one place where it was growing down to eye level. Up close you could see that the base of this "stuff" was a solid mass, and then growing out of that mass or base, were tightly clustered buds, each little bud with its own stem, almost like cauliflower. The stems were each about an inch to an inch and a half long. I reached out and put my hand on it. It was firm to the touch, again reminding me of the consistency of cauliflower, but somehow it just didn't look like a vegetable.

"I would be careful with that, Mr. McCarthy," Adair said. "There are some funny things that show up in caves sometimes. For all we know it could be poisonous or something."

"You're right, Mr. Adair. I'll be careful. You've never seen anything like this before?" I asked.

"Nope. Sure haven't. How about you, Will?"

"No sir. It's a new one on me," Will replied.

The three of us spent the next few minutes walking around the room in silence, examining the walls, looking at the "stuff".

Finally Adair said, "Well, it looks like this is where this tunnel ends. Fact is, we must be pretty close to the surface. There seems to be a little bit of light comin' in somewhere, which is mebbe why this stuff is growin' down here."

We looked carefully around the room. Adair was right. There was no continuance of the tunnel, at least that we could find, but there was a narrow crack in the ceiling toward the back of the room, letting a small amount of light in.

"I reckon we might as well head back," Adair said.

"I guess so," I replied. "I want to take a little of this stuff back with me and get it analyzed."

"What for," he asked?

"I'd like to find out what it is. It might be good to eat, like mushrooms. You like mushrooms?"

"Cain't say as I do," he replied, "but I reckon some folks do."

I took a pocket knife and a plastic bag out of my back pack, and cut several pieces of the "stuff" off of the wall, cutting as close as I could get to the base, to try and get as much of the stem as possible. Then I carefully placed the samples in the plastic bag. I decided to carry the bag in my hand rather than putting it back in the back pack, to keep the "stuff" from getting crushed on the way back out.

As we started back, I looked at my watch, curious about how long the trip back would take. It was now ten forty-five. We moved along much faster on the return trip, especially when we weren't in the narrow parts of the tunnel where the fall-off was, and when we reached the cave entrance it was twenty-five after eleven. It had taken just forty minutes to get back out.

We took the back-packs and miner's hats off and put them on Adair's pick-up truck.

"What do we do from here?" I asked.

"Well, as I say, we've seen about all there is to see, unless we can find another tunnel somewhere, and that'd have to be in that drop-off area. Let me think about that, and you think about it too, and then give me a call."

"I think I'd like to take one more look. We might find something."

"I understand how you feel. So far it ain't much of a cave I reckon, but on the other hand you got somethin' down there I never seen before."

"They say that sooner or later all the caves in these parts are somehow connected," Will Johnson said. "Over round Mammoth Cave they figure they's over three hundred miles of tunnels, all connected one way or another."

"Can you leave one of the lamps with me, Mr. Adair?"

"Fraid not, Mr. McCarthy. If you want to go back down in that cave, you call me. It's a lot more dangerous than you might think. You ever hear of Floyd Collins?"

I nodded. "There's a cave named after him."

"That's right," he said. "Floyd was an experienced caver, but I reckon he got over-confident or somethin'. Went down by hisself and got his foot caught. He died down there. You don't want no cave named after you, Mr. McCarthy. Least not that way."

There was no point in arguing, and I knew he was right. "O.K. But do me a favor. I'd appreciate it if you and Will didn't say anything to anyone just yet about what we found down there."

"Fair enough," he nodded. "We'll wait 'til we hear from you."

I settled up with him for the two days and they took off down the lane.

When I walked in the house Jennie looked up from a book.

"You're back early. How come?"

"It looks like we've run out of cave, maybe. But we did find something interesting."

I took the samples of the "stuff" out of the plastic bag and put them on the table in front or her.

"What is it?" she asked.

"I don't know, Jennie. Neither Adair or Johnson had ever seen anything like it before, but I'm curious about it." I paused. "We found this room down there, I guess it's roughly about the size of this house. The ceiling was covered solid with this stuff, and in some places it was growing down the sides of the walls. I guess we were up pretty close to the surface, and there was a little daylight filtering into the place from a crack somewhere in the ceiling. Adair thought that might account for this stuff growing there."

"That is weird," she said, looking at the vegetation lying there in front of her on the table.

"I'm going to have a beer. You want anything?"

She shook her head. "No thanks."

When I came back in the room, Jennie was nudging the "stuff" around on the table, and then I noticed she was chewing on something.

"Doesn't have much taste," she said.

My heart leaped! "My God, Jennifer! That stuff could be poisonous. We don't know anything about it. What the hell did you do that for?" I was more alarmed than angry, but she couldn't know that. As I said before, I usually called her Jennifer when I was mad about something.

She looked up at me, those big, green eyes welling up with tears, her face starting to flush. "I don't know, Brian. I never thought about it, I guess. Hell, I only ate one," she flashed back. "That couldn't possibly hurt anything. Besides it looks O.K.," she said defiantly.

I started to say "yeah, so do toad stools," but stopped. I think I had scared her enough. I went over to the couch, sat down next to her and put my arm around her "You're probably right, honey. I didn't mean to yell at you. We just ought to be careful until we know more about this stuff, that's all. So if you start to feel funny or sick or anything, tell me right away, O.K.?"

"I will," she nodded. "I'm sorry. I didn't mean to scare you."

"It'll be all right, babe. I think I'll put the rest of these in the refrigerator. They're used to a cooler temperature."

When I came back in the room, she had a serious look on her face. "Brian, I overheard the conversation you had with Adair about the lamp. I want you to promise me you won't go back in that cave alone."

"O.K. Jennie, I promise. By the way, when are you going to get over that cold you caught. I'm getting pretty horny, but I hate messing around with sickies."

She blew her nose again. "Why don't you see if you can latch on to one of the locals. It looks like there's a lot of action in Cave Junction."

I grinned, "Not a bad idea. I may go out cruising tonight."

Jennie held up one finger in a very impolite gesture. "You may end up sleeping in that frigging cave of yours," she said.

I was still a little worried about Jennie when we went to bed that night, but I had asked her several times during the evening how she felt, and she kept telling me she was all right. I sure hoped so.

Chapter Eight

I woke up the next morning and dressed quietly, trying not to disturb Jennie. I had decided to drive up to Louisville as early as possible and see if I could find a lab where I could get some testing done. This would probably turn out to be the classic wild goose chase of all time, but I had to find out, partly I guess because it was my cave. I would also be a lot less concerned about Jennie if I got a clean bill of health on this vegetation or whatever it was.

I went out to the kitchen and took the "stuff" out of the refrigerator. Maybe it was my imagination, but it seemed to have discolored slightly just over night.

Jennie was just stirring. "Feeling any better?" I asked.

She shook her head. "Not really, babe. I think I'll just stay in bed for a while. I may be dying," she croaked. "Weren't we supposed to have a meeting with Mr. Caldwell this morning?"

"Yeah. I'll have to call him and move it up to tomorrow."

I patted her on the head and told her of my plans for the day. "There's some ham and bread in the fridge if you get hungry. I should be back by late afternoon." I kissed her on the forehead, and was on my way.

When I got to the outskirts of Louisville I pulled into a gas station, full service, believe it or not, which was becoming an endangered species in Los Angeles. While they were taking care of the car I found a phone book and started looking for listings under "laboratories."

One company, Reynolds Laboratory, had a small space ad that looked promising. It read: Reynolds Laboratory, Agricultural and Industrial Testing and Analysis. That seemed to pretty well cover all the bases.

I dug what change I had out of my pocket, and dialed the number. The operator came on the line, "please deposit thirty cents." I did as instructed and the number rang. A pleasant, rather sexy female voice answered, slight southern accent.

"Good morning, Reynolds Labs."

"Good morning," I responded. "Is Mr. Reynolds in?"

"I'm sorry, there is no Mr. Reynolds with our company."

"I see. Could you tell me who's in charge?"

"Could you tell me how I can help you?" she inquired sweetly.

"I have an agricultural product I would like to get tested."

"Mr. Sievert is our general manager."

"Great. Can I talk to Mr. Sievert?"

"I'm sorry, Mr. Sievert is out of town. Could you hold for a moment please?" She went off the line, and was replaced shortly by the operator, who said "that will be an additional thirty cents, please."

What the hell. I made a snap decision that I had certainly received thirty cents worth of information so far from sweety-pie, so I fed another quarter and a nickel into the slots. My friend came back on the line.

"Who are you holding for?"

"I'm not real sure, doll. You were telling me that Mr. Sievert is out of town. Is there any one else I could talk to about some testing?"

"I'll put you through to his assistant."

"Who is that?" I asked.

"Mr. Barlow." She was getting a little testy.

"Thank you."

She came back on a minute later. "The line is busy."

"I'll wait."

After another minute or so she was back on the line. "Who are you waiting for?"

"Mr. Barlow."

"Oh yes, I can ring now."

A male voice came on the line. "Fred Barlow speaking," he said, in a thin, reedy voice.

"Mr. Barlow, my name is"- the operator was back on. "Thirty additional cents, please."

I reached in my pocket, but I was out of change. "I'll call you back," I shouted before the phone went dead.

I went over, paid for the gas, and got a couple of dollars in change. This time I got right through.

"Mr. Barlow, my name is Brian McCarthy. I'm visiting in this area from Los Angeles, and need to get an agricultural product tested rather quickly. Can you help me?"

He allowed as how he could, and I got directions from him. A half hour later I was at the Reynolds Laboratory, housed in an older two-story brown brick building in an industrial area, not far from downtown. I introduced myself to the receptionist. I thought I recognized her voice from our conversations. She was not bad looking, and was wearing a low cut dress that advertised a sensational set of jugs. I was ushered into Mr. Barlow's office, feeling a little silly carrying the plastic bag with the "stuff" in it.

Barlow was about five foot six, skinny as a rail, with curly red hair and horn rimmed glasses, and clearly showed the effects of a bad case of acne at some point in his youth. It seemed like everyone I'd met on this trip had come right out of central casting. Barlow was wearing what looked like a smock over his street clothes, and looked like he had been conceived and born in a laboratory.

He glanced quizzically at the bag I was carrying, shook my hand and asked, "How can I help you?"

I gave him just part of the story, omitting any details about where we had found it, other than to tell him it was down inside a cave. "I've never seen anything like it," I said, "and my associates," I liked that word, "and I would like to find out more about it. Is it edible, is is poisonous, does it have any food value, just what is it?"

Barlow took a pair of tweezers and picked up a piece of the "stuff," examining it, smelling it, and then setting it on a glass slide.

"It is different," Barlow said. Brilliant analysis. I thought.

"I think it has started to discolor somewhat," I observed, "although it has been refrigerated since we took it out of the cave, except for driving up here."

"Really?" He thought for a moment. "Well, if it came from a cave, it has been used to a constant temperature, probably in the low fifties. Perhaps we should refrigerate it now. Excuse me." He took the bag and walked out of the room, returning quickly.

"How long will it take to test it?" I asked.

"Oh, we should be able to start some preliminary testing this morning. What's your schedule?"

"The sooner the better. I should head back to the farm mid afternoon, and then back to Los Angeles toward the end of the week."

"Why don't you come back around two o'clock this afternoon. We'll go over what we have by then, and decide what to do from there."

"That sounds fine." I stood up. "By the way, do you have any idea of what the cost will be?"

He thought for a moment. "We're probably going to have about three hours work, at four hundred dollars an hour. Figure about twelve hundred dollars."

It seemed like a lot of money, but then I'd never dealt with a testing lab before, and I didn't want to screw around getting a second opinion somewhere else.

"O.K. I'll see you around two o'clock."

I stopped on my way out to talk to the receptionist. I leaned over the rail and flashed my biggest, most charming Irish smile. The view was sensational. "Do you have any idea where I might get some lunch around here?" I asked.

She smiled back. "There's nothing good around the office here. If you'll just drive down the street we're on for a mile or so toward downtown you'll come to the Metropole Restaurant. It's on the right hand side of the street. I think you'll enjoy that."

I kept smiling. "Thank you." I just wished Jennie could have been with me. She would have been furious.

It was still too early to eat, so I drove past the Metropole to the downtown area, a first for me, toured around for a while looking at the city, and then came back to the restaurant. I had a couple of leisurely beers and a pastrami sandwich, just killing time. After lunch I called Paul at the office, and got caught up on the business. I still hadn't told him anything about our adventures in the cave country, but did indicate that I would probably be back in the office in a day or two.

I got back to Reynolds Laboratories about a quarter of two. I told Miss Jugs that I had enjoyed the lunch, and that she had exquisite taste. It was a couple of minutes before Barlow came out to the lobby to get me, and I filled in the time by surreptitiously glancing at the receptionist. Then Barlow took me away from the view, back to a laboratory.

The laboratory was a large room filled with all kinds of equipment; sinks, burners, test tubes. It looked very scientific. There were a half a dozen technicians in laboratory frocks who seemed to be busy doing mysterious things. We went over to a table in the corner, where we sat down, and Barlow picked up some papers.

"Very interesting material, Mr. McCarthy."

"What do you think we have, Mr. Barlow?"

"Well, I'm not sure just exactly what it is, Mr. McCarthy, but there are some things we can tell you about it."

"Good."

"First of all, it isn't toxic. There doesn't appear to be anything in there that would be harmful to humans."

I smiled. "Frankly, Mr. Barlow, that's a relief. My fiancee chewed on a piece of the "stuff" before I had a chance to caution her, and I've been worried about her, although she seems to feel fine."

"I don't believe there's anything to be concerned about," Barlow said. "However, there is always the possibility of long term effects, particularly with repeated usage."

59

"Go on," I nodded.

"As far as food value, I don't think there is a great deal. However the substance does have an unusually high content of Vitamin C. There also appears to be a large amount of analgesics in it, as well."

"Analgesics?"

"Yes, more commonly known as aspirin, or aspirin-type medicines.

"I see."

"There is also a type of decongestant in it, as well as another substance we have been unable to identify. Very puzzling."

"Another substance?"

"Yes, something none of us have encountered before. We really don't know what to make of it. We think it would take some extensive testing to determine the exact nature of the substance."

"What does it all add up to, Mr. Barlow?"

"I really can't tell you, not without further testing, Mr. McCarthy. The vegetation, I guess we can call it that, may not be anything at all. Just different. But we were able to provide you with data on the two things you asked about, regarding it being poisonous or not and the food value content."

He selected a test tube out of a rack in front of him. It contained a black substance at the bottom.

"We took a sample of the substance and subjected it to heat. It doesn't like heat at all. It just sort of shriveled up and turned black almost immediately. I think we were right when we decided to refrigerate it this morning." He hesitated. "I guess that's about it."

"Well, thank you for the prompt service, Mr. Barlow. How much do I owe you?"

He picked up a piece of paper on the desk in front of him, and handed it to me. It was an invoice for twelve hundred dollars. I shook my head slightly.

"If you'll remember, Mr. McCarthy, I told you our standard fee was four hundred dollars an hour. We spent three hours on your project, and did give you very prompt service."

"That's true." I handed him one of my cards. "I'd like to run the invoice through the office. Would you mind billing this to us out in California?"

"Not at all. We'll send the written report with the bill as well. Let me get the unused substance." He disappeared out a door, then reappeared with a plastic container. There were a couple of stalks, or whatever you'd call them, of the "stuff" in the bottom of the container.

"Just what do you plan to do with this substance, Mr. McCarthy?"

"Mr. Barlow, I don't have the foggiest idea."

We shook hands and I left, smiling at Miss Jugs on my way out. She was still looking good.

I hit the afternoon traffic getting out of Louisville, and got back to the farm a little after five. Jennie was sitting in front of the fireplace, her faithful Kleenex box close at hand.

"Hi, Babe. Feeling any better?"

She shrugged. "About the same. How was the trip?"

"Good. I found a lab up there that was able to give me some fast analysis, and I found out five things. One, the "stuff" is apparently harmless, so I guess you're going to live. Two, it doesn't have much food value. Three, it has a lot of Vitamin C, aspirin, and something else they couldn't identify. Four, it definitely doesn't like heat. And five, we are in the wrong business. The bill was twelve hundred dollars. Oh, yes, and six, the lab has a receptionist who just may have the best set of jugs in Louisville."

Jennie stuck out her tongue at me. "Big deal."

I grinned. "Also I talked to Paul. Everything's O.K. at the office."

"Speaking of the office, I'm starting to atrophy," Jennie said. "When are we going home?"

"Soon, my love. I'll meet Caldwell tomorrow morning, and finish up with him, and we'll see if we can get a plane back tomorrow afternoon. O. K? If I have to come back later I can come back here by myself."

"Yeah, as long as you stay away from that lab up in Louisville."

I smiled. She hadn't forgotten the remark I had made about Miss Jugs. "Why Jennie, what a distrustful thing to say."

I went out to the kitchen to grab a beer and saw the "stuff" sitting there in the plastic container. I grabbed a small plate and a salt-shaker and walked back in the living room. "Let's see what this tastes like with a little salt on it," I said, and dumped the two remaining pieces on the plate and sprinkled them with salt. I offered one to Jennie, which she took, and I ate the other. Even with salt on it, the "stuff" was quite bland, not distasteful, it was just bland.

"What do you think?"

"It's saltier," Jennie said.

"Thanks a lot. I guess what we've got here is something you can't cook, because the damned stuff turns black almost instantly under heat, and it doesn't have much flavor of its own, so I guess we aren't going to revolutionize the snack food industry. Oh, well. Back to advertising."

Jennie sneezed again, and reached for another Kleenex.

She went to bed early, feeling terrible. I threw a couple of logs in the fireplace, got them burning, and sat in front of the fire for a while, thinking of the past few days. So many things had happened, the letter from Caldwell, the excitement of finding the cave and exploring it, and now everything seemed sort of anti-climactic. I knew the cave wasn't going to be the ninth wonder of the world. There wasn't enough to see down there, and the rooms we had found were too hard to get too, so unless we came up with something else, I had to admit to myself that there wasn't any point in hanging on to the farm and cave just so I could own it. The solution seemed to be to tell Caldwell to bring in his buyer and unload it. My immediate problem was that I didn't have any idea of what the property was worth. I thought about that for a while, and decided I might be able to get some advice from Jim Adair. He should have some idea of what farms were going for in the area.

I decided I would call Adair in the morning anyway and see if he was willing to take one more shot at the cave. I owed myself at least that much, and finally went to bed, feeling sort of let down. I spent a restless night, and at one point dreamt I was down in the cave with Miss Jugs. We were trying to hide from Merton Caldwell, who apparently was trying to do us bodily harm. Finally I dropped off into a deep sleep.

I woke up groggily, feeling Jennie shaking my shoulder. "Brian, Brian! Wake up." She was excited about something.

"What's the matter, Jennie?" I said, still not quite awake.

"It's gone it's gone!" Jennie said, almost yelling.

"What's gone? What's the matter?"

"My cold, Brian! It's gone, completely gone! No fever, no runny nose, no sore throat, it's all gone!"

"That's great, Jennie," I muttered, still not understanding.

"Brian, don't you understand? There's no way this cold could be gone this fast. You know how long it takes me to get over one. I probably had at least another week to go, and all of a sudden it's gone. I've been lying here trying to figure out. It must be the "stuff." It's a miracle!"

I sat up in bed. "What? Really? You're sure?"

"What else could it be?"

I looked at Jennie. She looked good, sounded good, and obviously felt good.

"My God!" I exclaimed as it started too sink in. "What if it is. What if the "stuff" turns out to be an overnight remedy for the common cold! My God!"

"It has to be, Brian. I really feel great! Oh my Lord, I'm starting to sound like a TV commercial." she laughed.

My mind started playing with the possibilities. It could be an instant cure for the cold. No more pills, no more cough medicine, no more doctor visits, no more time off work, it was mind boggling. "Good Lord, Jennie. We'll be zillionaires. Can you imagine the potential this could have?"

By this time I had also gotten around to looking at Jennie, bouncing around in the bed in her flimsy negligee.

"You know what else is great, Jennie? You're not a sickie any more!"

She stopped bouncing. "You know what? You're absolutely right."

I reached out for her, and what few clothes we had on were thrown on the floor in seconds, and we were rolling on the bed, touching each other everywhere, almost in a frenzy. Maybe it was the excitement we were going through because of the "stuff", and what is had apparently done for Jennie, but the session we had that morning was something else.

Every once in a wile I think back to my marriage to Lila. What a mess!

Lila wasn't bad looking. In fact she was pretty attractive. We met in a bar up in Hollywood one night, and that was the start of our relationship, which got pretty hot pretty fast.

Lila was trying to break into the movies, with a notable lack of success. The next thing I knew I had proposed to her, and we were married, a quickie in one of those Vegas Chapels, with an Elvis look-a-like standing beside us for pictures.

That's when things started to go bad. It seemed like every time I got home there would be another package on the bed, another dress, another pair of shoes, another something. Next thing I knew, my two credit cards were maxed out.

I told her she was going to have to slow down, and she replied, "that's not what I married you for, Buddy."

A few days later I found an expensive gold chain on our dresser.

"What the Hell is this?" I demanded.

"Don't worry about it. I didn't buy it."

"Then where did it come from?"

"A friend."

"A friend? What does that mean?"

"Oh, you know. An admirer."

I had noticed that all of her recent 'auditions' seemed to be occurring at night, late at night. This was the last straw. I packed up the next morning and moved out.

Then I called a lawyer friend of mine, Johnny Ferguson. I explained the circumstances to him. "Johnny, you've got to get me out of this, and as cheaply as possible. This broad's already got me in the poor house."

He got the job done, but not all that cheaply. By comparison Jennie was so great. We are just going to have to set a date. Soon. I don't want her to get away.

The rain continued to pour down outside, and I could hear it on the roof, and now I could hear the rush of the water in the creek, just a few feet from the house. If it came up too much higher we could be in real trouble. I wondered if my cousin had ever had this problem during the many years he had lived here.

Chapter Nine

I got up and got dressed quietly. Jennie likes to doze off again sometimes when we've made love in the morning, and she had drifted off to sleep again.

I needed to get some more samples to take back to Los Angeles. Then we'd figure out a way to get it back home under refrigeration. Probably one of those little party things you carry beer and ice in would do, anything that would maintain it at a temperature somewhere around fifty-four degrees.

The important thing now was to get back home. There was no need to talk to Caldwell about selling the place. Sell a gold mine? I also wasn't going to worry about exploring the cave any more for the time being. That could wait for another day.

Common sense and my conscience told me I shouldn't be going down into that cave by myself. I knew darn well what Jim Adair would say, and I had promised Jennie I wouldn't go in there. Aw, what the hell. I had to get the samples to take back home, and there was no point in bothering Adair just for a quick trip back to where the "stuff" was. I looked at my watch. Seven thirty-five. If I hurried I would be back close to nine, and Jennie would probably just be getting up. I knew she would be really pissed if she knew what I was about to do, and probably would be even when she found out after the fact, but I sure as hell wasn't going to tell her in advance. I knew all I would get would be a lot of static.

I had put new batteries and a bulb in the flashlight, and stuck a couple of spare batteries in my jacket pocket, then eased my way quietly out the back door. I took along a knife and the plastic container they had given me at Reynolds lab to put the samples in.

I went into the cave and was lowering myself over the rock pile where the slide had occurred when my foot slipped, and I grabbed at some of the rocks to keep myself from falling. Deja vu! It was the same exact thing I had done the other day to start the landslide. How stupid can you be? At first, a few rocks rolled down the pile, and then I heard an ominous rumble. Rocks of all sizes began cascading out of the crevice. I rolled away from the falling rocks, back into the cave and covered my face with my arms until the noise stopped.

When it was finally quiet and the rocks had stopped falling, I opened my eyes, and saw nothing but darkness. The opening was completely closed! My first thought was the flashlight and I groped around frantically in the dark until I found it. I pushed the button, pointing it at the rock pile, and what I saw in front of me now was a solid wall from floor to ceiling. In fact, it continued going on up into the crevice as far as I could see. There was no telling how many feet thick the wall was. I was sealed in!

"Damn it, McCarthy! You bloody, stupid idiot," I yelled at myself. I don't think I had ever been as angry at my own stupidity as I was at that moment. I had gone into the cave alone, knowing damned well that I shouldn't have. On top of that, I'd already been partly trapped in the cave once, and knew that Adair had been concerned about the rock-slide area. Obviously there had been good reason for his concern.

I was trapped. Trapped in the cave without food or water, or even adequate clothing. I had on jeans, a woolen shirt, a jacket and had only put on one pair of socks. That was O.K. for the quick trip I had planned, but not for a prolonged stay.

Hell, I had been taught in survival training that you always plan for the worst thing that can happen. They also taught you that under stress, the first thing you do is to calm down and take inventory, so I decided to do just that.

I was also concerned about that sharp pain I had felt in my right ankle, so I got slowly to my feet and put a little weight on my right foot. It hurt a little, but seemed to be able to bear my weight, so I started walking around until I was satisfied that it was O.K. Nothing was broken, just a little sore. Feeling better about that, I began to think things over. It shouldn't take Jennie too long to figure out what happened. The car was still in the driveway, so when I didn't show up, she'd decide that I might have gone back to the cave, despite my promise that I wouldn't. Then once she saw the cave-in she would go and get some help. Boy, I could hear her now, once I got out of this mess.

I felt myself starting to get angry again. Stay cool, McCarthy. Speaking of which, I was starting to feel the chilly temperature in the cave. I figured I would be able to last without food and water until they dug me out, which I guessed would be in a day or two. In the meantime, the main thing was to keep from getting too cold, so I got up, and moved around, flapping my arms until I started to warm up. I'd just have to exercise occasionally, and everything should be O.K.

It's incredible how slowly time passes when you have nothing to do but sit and think, enveloped in that inky, black darkness. I tried to focus my mind on various things that would help pass the time. I started out by trying to concentrate on our financial problems at the agency, but under the present circumstances, they seemed very remote and insignificant.

Then I started thinking about Jennie, and what an fantastic lady she is. Since we had just made love a few hours ago I still had this vivid picture of her body in my mind, and I thought about that for a while. Jennie has these gorgeous long legs, and has a set of boobs to die for, and of course that beautiful face. But the more I thought about it the clearer it became to me that our relationship was more, a lot more, than just sex, as good as that was, and I concluded that if I got out of here - when I got out of here, think positive, McCarthy, - I was going to ask her to marry me. It was time to do that anyway.

I started trying to plan the wedding, presuming that she would accept, but since I had no family and she had very few relatives, it wouldn't be a very big crowd. Jennie and I didn't have a lot of close friends. It seemed like we were wrapped up in the business most of the time. Then, when we could, we liked to get away on weekends, getting down to the desert for golf, or up the coast on little trips. We just didn't socialize all that much, which suited us just fine, plus we both liked movies, and went whenever we could. It wasn't that we were really loners or anti-social, but we were happy with each other and what we were doing.

As far as the wedding, I thought facetiously, we could always go up to Las Vegas for one of those quickie ceremonies, complete with videotape, an Elvis look-alike and a coupon for the slot machines, but that had always seemed a little tacky to me. Besides, I had done that with Lila, which certainly hadn't worked out well at all.

Then I had my first hunger pang, and then all I could think about was a big juicy hamburger, medium rare, with a thick slice of Bermuda onion, slathered with ketchup and accompanied by an ice-cold bottle of Foster's beer. The beer almost sounded better than the hamburger. I knew this wasn't doing me any good, so I tried thinking of other things, but the beer and the hamburger kept floating back into my mind.

It seemed like hours had gone by, and I switched the flashlight on briefly to take another look at my watch. Twelve fifty-six. Just a little over an hour since the last time I had looked, and I had been down in the cave now for about five hours. I got up and exercised again to ward off the cold, and then sat back down. Sure was quiet.

"Sing something, McCarthy," I said out loud.

"Well, I'll try," I replied to myself, "but I really have a terrible singing voice."

"It's O.K. McCarthy. Who the hell's going to criticize?"

I started off with some raunchy songs from my youth, old favorites like "She wore Her Nightie" and "Sittin' on O'Reilly's Porch." That cheered me up for a while, and brought back some distant memories, but I soon ran out of requests, and lapsed back into silence.

Suddenly, in that total quiet, I heard a faint noise, barely perceptible, like something scratching, coming from not far away, or so it seemed, but it was on this side of the cave-in, on my side. I scrambled for a minute locating the flashlight, and then turned it on.

Those damned rats were back! There, just a yard or so away from my feet were three of the ugliest rats I've ever seen. God I hate rats! I shuddered involuntarily, yelled at them, and then picked up a stone next to me and threw it at them. It glanced off one of them and they scurried back down the cave until they were out of sight. I shuddered again. Rats! Ugh!

I had to turn the flashlight off pretty quickly to conserve the batteries, but then I sat there in the dark, wondering where they were now. How had they gotten in the cave? Had they come in the way I had, or from some other entrance of their own? How many of them were there? Would they be back? Were they hungry?

My mind flashed back to a short story I had read when I was a kid, one I had always remembered, about a man who was all alone in a lighthouse, isolated on a desolate coast. An abandoned ship crashed on the rocks at the base of the lighthouse, pushed there by a storm. To his horror, as the ship broke up on the rocks below the lighthouse keeper saw hundreds of rats jump from it onto the tiny little isthmus of land the lighthouse had been built on. It was soon apparent that they were starving, and they began to attack the building, gnawing at the window frames, at the doors, determined to get at him. The writer painted a vivid picture of all those scratching, screeching animals, clawing to get in at the lighthouse keeper, staring at him through the windows as he moved higher and higher into the lighthouse. Finally his rescuers towed a barge past the island with raw meat on it, and the rats swam off the lighthouse toward it, and were eaten by the sharks. It was something like that.

I had no idea under what circumstances a pack of rats would actually attack a human being, but that story came back to me vividly as I sat there, and I thought I ought to make some kind of preparation for war, including conservation of the flashlight batteries, so I'd have some light when and if I needed it.

Still sparing the batteries, I groped in the darkness in the area around me, accumulating a pile of rocks for ammunition, and I had plenty of rocks. I decided that my strategy would be to turn on the flashlight briefly every few minutes to see if the rats were coming back. I would probably be all right if there weren't too many of them, and if they'd already had a decent breakfast. Also, if I sat quietly I'd most likely be able to hear them if and when they came back.

Every time I turned on the flashlight to check for rats I'd glance at my watch. It was about a half hour later when I saw them again, but this time there were four or five of them. I wasn't really crazy about the trend. I threw a couple of more rocks at them, but they were keeping their distance, and ran back down the tunnel again, which maybe was a good sign. Hopefully they were there out of curiosity, not hunger.

I kept that routine up for the next hour or so, and didn't see the rats again during that period of time. It was about two o'clock when I heard the four taps, coming from the other side of the rock-slide, a brief silence, and then four more taps. My heart leaped! Help had arrived!

I picked up a stone, went over to the rock pile and returned their signal, hitting the rock four times, pausing and then tapping four more times. They repeated the signal a few seconds later. Now it was only a matter of time! I had made contact with the rescue party.

I just hoped that, before they got me out, there wasn't going to be a problem with my furry friends, crawling around in the darkness down there. God, I hated the thought! I never could stand rats under any circumstances, the few times I had seen them, and being down here alone in the cold and the dark with them was much worse. I decided the next time they showed up I'd chase them back down the cave, at least to the fork, and see which way they went. It occurred to me than that as long as I was trapped down in cave I might as well go back into the room and cut off the samples I needed to take back to Los Angeles. That was why I had come down here in the first place. Hopefully the rats would take the left fork, and would not be waiting up there for me when I took the right tunnel back to the "stuff". In fact I wasn't so sure that if they took the right tunnel that I'd be able to go back in there, crawling on my hands and knees, knowing that they might be up ahead somewhere.

While I was up I did some more exercises to keep warm, and then sat back down. I must have dozed off after that, and was awakened by something crawling on my leg. I yelled and jumped to my feet, and then groped for the flashlight on the ground. When I finally got it on, there were several rats, only a few feet away. This was getting serious. I picked up some rocks, threw a couple at them, and began yelling and waving my arms at them. They turned around and scampered back down the cave. I followed them to where the tunnel forked, and to my relief they all took the tunnel going off to the left. Hopefully I wouldn't encounter any of them going back to get some more samples.

I decided to keep on going and get it over with. I went quickly back to the rock pile, grabbed the plastic container and moved through the tunnel as quickly as I could, at least under those conditions, flicking on the flashlight every few seconds until I got to the area where I had to get down and crawl. I sure would like to have had a pair of knee crawlers, but I moved through that part of the cave as rapidly as I could anyway.

I moved very slowly thru the fall-off area, knowing that if I slipped, it was all over. No one would know what had happened to me until they found my body, whenever that would be.

When I got to the room where the vegetation was growing, I cut off about forty stalks of the "stuff", filling up the plastic container I had brought. I also saw what appeared to be the start of a new growth, some tiny stubs where I had cut off the samples before, so the "stuff" apparently was able to regenerate itself, and maybe fairly quickly, which was interesting news.

I returned back to the rock-slide area, still using the flashlight sparingly. So far it was holding up, and I did have that set of spare batteries with me, but I had no idea how long it would take for the rescuers to dig me out. I had the feeling that the rats would return, and I sure as hell didn't want to be down there in the cave with them without some kind of light.

On top of everything else I started sneezing, and began to get that funny tickle in my nose that you get when you're starting to catch a cold. Just what I needed! "Wait a minute, Brian," I said.

"You've got the world's greatest cold remedy right here with you." I took a couple of stalks out of the container and munched on them slowly. The "stuff" might be great for curing colds, but it would never replace a cheeseburger and a cold beer.

I felt myself starting to get angry again. Stay cool, McCarthy. Speaking of which, I was starting to feel the chill. I figured I would be able to last without food and water until they dug me out, which I guessed would be in a day or two. In the meantime, the main thing was to keep from getting too cold, so I moved around, flapping my arms until I started to warm up. I'd just have to exercise occasionally, and everything should be O.K. I quickly cut off the samples I needed, and headed back to the rock pile.

I sat back down, resting my back against a large rock, and the next thing I knew I had drifted off to sleep.

✳✳✳

Jennie woke up and slowly stretched. She still felt warm and cozy from the sex with Brian, smiling as she thought about it. She still couldn't believe what had happened to her cold.

"Brian?" She waited. No answer. She got up, threw on some panties, a bra, blue jeans and a pull-over sweater, and walked out into the kitchen. She saw the empty coffee cup and put the water back on to heat.

She walked outside. The car was sitting in the driveway. "He's probably poking around that cave again," she said to herself. The kettle began to steam and she went back in, put a teaspoon of instant coffee in a cup and poured the boiling water over it.

"He wouldn't have gone back in there by himself," she said. She remembered that Brian had put a flashlight down somewhere. She looked quickly through the house but couldn't find it. She seemed to remember it being on the table out in the kitchen, but it wasn't there now.

"Maybe it's in the car," she thought as she quickly slipped on some socks and shoes, grabbed the car keys off of the dresser and walked out to the car. She looked inside, under the seats and in the trunk. No flashlight. Then she went back in the house, grabbed a pack of matches and came back outside again.

"Brian," she yelled, and then waited. Silence. "Where are you?" Silence again. She started back along the creek toward the cave. The water was down now to the point where it was no longer really dangerous, just a foot or so deep, but she still moved carefully along the bank. She reached the entrance to the cave and peered in.

"Brian?" she yelled again. No answer. She advanced a few steps into the cave and then stopped to light a match. When the light flared up she saw the solid pile of rocks in front of her.

"Oh my God!" she said. "The cave's closed in!" She dropped the match as it started to singe her finger, and lit another one, and looked for a moment at the solid wall. Somehow she was sure he was in there. "Brian, can you hear me?" she yelled. "Are you in there?" Had Brian been awake he might have been able to faintly hear Jennie's voice on the other side of the wall, just a few feet away.

"I know he's in there. I've got to get help!" she said. "God, sometimes he's just like a little kid, running off and doing things without even thinking about it. Damn him!" She was angry and scared.

She ran out of the cave, and started moving quickly back along the bank, and in her haste to get back to the house, she got careless for a second. She set her left foot down on a loose rock, which suddenly gave way. Her foot plunged down, she lost her balance, and fell part way into the cold muddy water. It was the same foot she had injured the other day, and it didn't do it any good.

She managed to pull herself out of the creek, back up onto the bank. "Got to get help," she said through clenched teeth, and slowly edged her way along the bank. She was soaking wet, and starting to shake from the cold and the shock, but she kept inching along until she was finally able to crawl up onto level ground.

Just as she finally reached the kitchen door, she remembered. "Damn it, there's no telephone in the house!"

She got to the bedroom, sat on the bed, and began to peel off the wet clothes. She used the bedspread to towel off, dragged out some dry clothes and got dressed. She was starting to feel a little warmer now.

"Got to get to the car," she thought. She reached into the pocked of the wet jeans, and felt nothing. "Oh God, where are the car keys?" She searched frantically in the other pocket, but found nothing. "They must have dropped in the creek when I fell in." Tears of frustration ran down her cheeks. "Son of a bitch," she swore out loud. "Got to get help for Brian."

With a sigh of relief she finally reached the mail box out on the main road, and propped herself up against it. It was not a heavily traveled road, but she had heard cars going by occasionally the past couple of days, and knew eventually that some one would come along.

Finally she heard the noise of an engine off in the distance, and saw a car approaching. She waved the stick at it. As it went by she saw an older couple in the front seat and two children in the back. They didn't slow down.

"Stop!" she screamed. "For God's sake, stop!" She could see the two children waving at her through the back window as the car continued to move away from her down the road. The tears started again. "Damn it! Won't you bastards stop?"

It seemed like a long time before she heard another engine. This time she saw a pick-up truck coming toward her on her side of the road.

"I'll stop this one," she said.

As the truck neared she began waving her arms, and then let her body drop down on the road. The truck veered to the left to miss her and then screeched to a stop.

An older man in overalls, a heavy wool jacket and a baseball cap came around the side of the truck.

"What the hell's the matter with you, lady?"

She looked up at him. "Help me, please. My friend is trapped back in a cave."

Concern immediately crossed his face. "O.K., O.K. Take it easy, ma'am. Let's get you in the truck and over to Doc Adams."

"I don't need a doctor. You've got to get a hold of Mr. Adair. He knows about the cave."

"Jim Adair?"

Jennie nodded.

"All right, ma'am, I know Jim Adair. I'll call him from the Doc's. Let's git you in the truck."

"Easy does it, ma'am. You're goin' to be O.K. The Doc's place is only about ten minutes from here."

She felt the car slowing, and opened her eyes as it pulled off the road into a driveway, and up to a small red brick house. The sign on the front lawn read "George D. Adams, M. D."

The man honked his horn several times as they pulled to a stop. The door of the house opened and a elderly man walked out.

"Hi Doc. Got a woman here who was out in the road in front of the Thomas place. Says she's got a friend trapped back in a cave. Wants me to call Jim Adair."

"You've got to help Brian. He's in a cave out back of the house."

"The Thomas house?" the Doctor asked.

"Yes. You've got to get him out," she said.

✳✳✳

I woke up with a start, and it took a few seconds for me to realize where I was. The first thing that struck me was the utter silence and the total darkness. I had sort of been aware of it when I had gone down into the cave with Jim Adair and Will Johnson. It was all around you, but there had always been a light on of some kind and a couple of other people with you. Now I was experiencing what total darkness was really like. I moved my hand to where I knew it was right in front of my eyes and wiggled my fingers, but I couldn't see a thing.

And as I sat there the silence became uncanny. After a few minutes I could hear my heart beating, and I don't think I had ever noticed that sound before in my life.

Also I was becoming chilled. I felt around until I found the flashlight, and then stood up, and began moving my arms and legs until the warmth came back. I turned on the flashlight for a second, and looked at my watch. Nine forty-eight. I had slept for over an hour. I turned the light off quickly, deciding that I had better conserve the batteries as much as possible, even though I had a second set in my jacket pocket.

I started thinking about what was going on outside the cave. Had Jennie found the rock-slide yet? Had she called Adair? Was he even around? Maybe he'd gone away for the weekend. "Stop fussing, McCarthy," I told myself. "She'll get some help somewhere."

I wondered if I would be able to hear them when they started clearing the rocks away. How bad was the rock-slide? How long would it take for them to break through that wall of rock?

Easy does it, Brian. Stay relaxed. They're going to get you out. But where were they?

Chapter Ten

By the time they found Jim Adair and he got over to Doc Adam's, it was almost one o'clock in the afternoon. The receptionist took him back to the Doctor's office.

"Hello, Doc. How's the woman doin'?"

"She's all right."

"I was over there the other day, helpin' this fella go down in a cave he found. Name's Brian McCarthy, from Los Angeles. I guess he inherited the place from Joe Thomas. Wasn't much of a cave, but we did find some funny stuff down there." He stopped. "I'm not supposed to say anything about that."

"What kind of stuff?"

"I don't know, Doc. It was some weird stuff just growin' in a room down in the cave. This fella McCarthy, he asked me not to say anything about it, and I forgot. So just forget I said anything, O.K.? Anyway, let's go look at the woman."

Doctor Adams led the way back to a room and Jim Adair looked down at Jennie, who was napping. "Yep, that's her. Pretty thing, ain't she. Well, I guess I'd better get on over to the cave. Will Johnson's waitin' out in the truck."

When they got over to the farm Adair and Johnson took the two back-packs out of the truck, two picks, two crowbars and a large battery-powered torch. There were some extra supplies that they left in the truck.

As soon as they stepped into the tunnel, Adair turned on the torch, and saw the rock pile. He shook his head, looking at the blocked tunnel.

"I was afraid that this was what happened, Will. I didn't like the looks of that crevice when we went through there before. I thought there might be a whole bunch of rocks back up in there."

They walked over to the rock pile, and Adair directed the torch up at the ceiling. "No tellin' how much rock is still up there," Adair said, "but it's gonna take a while to clear that out. Could be two or three days, maybe even longer than that."

Will shrugged his shoulders, shaking his head. "Looks like a big job to me."

"Best thing is to go in from the other entrance, the one Joe found back in the woods. Once we get in the cave I'm sure we can find him. Ain't all that big a cave. Hope that fella McCarthy's O.K. Darn fool!"

He went back to the cave entrance, picked up the crowbar and brought it back to the roc-slide. He aimed the blunt end of it at a large rock up near the top and struck it four times. He paused, hit it four more times, and then waited.

"Let's see if he's in there somewhere. He should be able to hear that. If he's O.K., that is."

"Listen!' said Will Johnson.

They heard a faint sound from the other side. Four taps, a pause and then four more.

"O.K., he's in there, Will. I'll answer him back and then let's get out of here and tell somebody what we're planning on doing."

***

I wondered if I would be able to hear them when they started clearing the rocks away. How bad was the slide? How long would it take for them to break through that wall of rock?

Easy does it, Brian. Stay relaxed. They're going to get you out. But where were they?

The next time I turned on the flashlight there were at least a dozen rats in sight, some of them about ten feet or so away. They seemed to be getting braver. I yelled at them and threw some more rocks at them until they scampered out of sight. The beam from the flashlight was getting dimmer, and it wouldn't be long before I would have to use the second set of batteries. My watch said twelve fourteen.

About two o'clock the first set of batteries gave out while I was looking for rats again. I replaced them with the second set, wondering how long they would last and promising not to use them any more than I absolutely had to. Hopefully they would last until some one got me out of here. The rats showed up again about two thirty.

"Don't you guys ever sleep, for Christ's sake?" I pelted them with a couple of more rocks. "You're getting to be a real pain in the butt. What I wouldn't give for a shot gun."

***

Jim Adair got to the other cave entrance with his sidekick about quarter of four. He had taken the time to call Doc Adams, and told him to let Jennie know that they had made contact with McCarthy, and that they would be getting him out shortly.

Once they were in the cave Jim stopped and studied things carefully. He and Will had both lit their headlamps. After a couple of minutes he pointed to the right.

"I believe we want to go that way to get to where Brian's stuck."

"All right Jim." The cave was slanting down slowly until they came to a split in the tunnel. Jim pointed down the tunnel going to the right.

"I believe that's the way we would go if we wanted to find that funny stuff. We'll try the other way."

They headed off in that direction, picking their way slowly along the rock-strewn path. After about thirty minutes, Jim stopped.

"I see something up ahead, Will. I think we're coming to the rock-slide that had closed down the cave.

His flashlight pointed at a solid wall of rocks.

"Mr. McCarthy," he yelled out and listened for a moment.

I heard the voice and stood up where Adair could see me. "I'm over here Mr. Adair," I said.

"Mr. McCarthy, you O, K.?"

"I'm just fine Mr. Adair, but I'm sure glad to see you. Did you come in the other away?"

"That's right. You're safe now."

"I guess I caused you a lot of trouble."

Adair was not smiling, and he looked levelly at me.

"You're a damned fool, Mr. McCarthy. I thought you and me had talked about goin' into a cave alone."

Now that he knew that he had me out of there safely, he was really pissed off. It was the first time I'd seen him show any emotion.

I looked at him and nodded slowly. "You're right, Mr. Adair. And I'm really sorry, I want to talk to you about compensating everyone for their time, and I'd like a chance to try to explain this to you later." We walked back to the cave entrance without any conversation and I looked around. "Where's Jennie?"

"She's down at Doc Adams. She hurt her ankle tryin' to get help for you.

"Oh my God!" That made me feel pretty small. "Is she O.K.?"

"She's about as good as she could be, I reckon," Adair replied. "No thanks to you."

"Where is she?"

"They took her over to Doc Adam's place when she was hurt. She's still over there."

We walked back slowly to the house. Adair handed me a set of car keys when we got there. "These yours?"

I nodded.

"One of the boys found them on the bank of the creek?"

"I wonder how they got there?" I stuck them in my pocket. "What can I do for you and the men who dug me out?"

"Stay out of the cave, Mr. McCarthy," he said grimly, still not smiling.

I tried to grin and held up my right hand. "I promise, Mr. Adair, but I'd like to come over this afternoon to see you if you're going to be around. I want to explain what happened and why I went back in the cave, and also talk to you about a couple of other things. Is that OK?"

He looked up at me, frowning. "Yeah, I reckon I'll be around."

"I've got to pick up Jennie first. I'll come over about three o'clock."

I stuck out my hand. He looked at it for a minute and then shook it, and gave me directions on how to get to Doc Adam's place. As soon as Adair and Will were gone I went inside, jumped in the tub, changed my clothes and headed for the doctor's office.

Jennie was up and dressed, and broke into tears when she saw me. "Brian McCarthy, you big dumb idiot!" she said. "I ought to break your neck!"

I kissed her gently. "I know, Jennie. I'm really sorry, honey. Let's get you back to the farm." I settled up with the doctor, and helped her into the car.

"God, I feel awful about this," I said, nodding at her foot. "How are you doing?"

"You caused everybody a lot of trouble," she said, ignoring my question. Like Adair, once she knew I was safe, she was angry. "You promised me you wouldn't go back in that cave alone.

It was starting to sink in. "But what if it is! What if the "stuff" really turns out to be an overnight remedy for the common cold! My God!"

"It has to be, Brian. I really feel great! She laughed.

"I know, Jennie. It was a stupid thing to do, and I've already been chewed out by Adair. All I can say is I'm sorry."

You know that feeling you have when you're absolutely wrong, and you feel like you're six inches high? I really felt terrible about her ankle, because it was obviously my fault in the first place. The Doc had said that the ankle wasn't as serious a strain as it could have been. As we drove back over to the house she told me what had happened to her. When we got back there, I got her settled down on the couch, and sat down beside her.

She looked at me and asked, "What now, Brian?"

"Jennie, we've found something here that may be incredible, not only medically but financially. I started to get a cold myself down in the cave, so I went back to that room, got some of the "stuff", and ate a couple of pieces. It snapped me right out of it. Have you had any after effects?"

"Yeah, I hurt my ankle."

I laughed. "No, seriously, Jennie."

"No, I really haven't. Everything seems to be fine. I'm a little groggy from yesterday, but I don't think that has anything to do with the "stuff". The cold is definitely gone."

"Jennie, my love, we are about to make medical history. And I'd like to do something to make it up to you for your broken ankle and for causing you all this trouble."

"It's not broken, Brian. What'd you have in mind? It had better be good!"

"I want you to marry me."

Jennie's eyes got big and teary, and she threw her arms around me.

"That is very good," she whispered in my ear. "Consider yourself forgiven."

It's amazing the things some girls can do, even with a bad ankle.

Chapter Eleven

That afternoon, after Jennie and I had a late lunch, at the Diner of course, I drove over to see Jim Adair. Jennie was kind of grumpy and stayed home. However, I had made arrangements for us to fly back to Los Angeles the next morning, and that had cheered her up.

Jim Adair walked out of his house as I came up the driveway.

He nodded at me and said. "How's Jennie?"

"She's doing O.K.," I replied. He just sort of grunted, still not being terribly friendly.

"Mr. Adair, first of all let me apologize again for the trouble I caused. I know it was a damned fool thing to do, and I'm really sorry, but I'd like to explain something to you.

"I'm listening," he said, hands on hips.

"First of all, however, let me say two things. What I am about to tell you must remain in absolute confidence, and secondly, I am going to need some help from you."

"Well, as far as the confidential part, you got my word on that, but as far as the help part, it depends on just what it is you want."

"O. K., that's fair. Let's take it one thing at a time. Do you remember that when you first met Jennie she had a very bad cold? She was sneezing, had a sore throat and a runny nose?"

"I believe I recollect that, Mr. McCarthy."

"Well, take my word for it that it should have taken at least another week for Jennie to get over it. But she ate some of the "stuff" that we found down in the cave, and it cured her overnight. The cold was completely gone the next morning. There was not a trace of it left, sore throat, runny nose, coughing, all of it gone. Just like that, a week before it should have happened." I snapped my fingers for emphasis. "Also, when I was trapped down there in the cave, I started feeling like I was catching cold, so I ate some of the 'stuff', and apparently it stopped my cold, too."

Adair looked skeptical.

"Mr. Adair," I continued, "I took some of that vegetation, whatever it is, up to Louisville last Friday and had it tested. The laboratory told me that it is harmless as far as being poisonous or anything like that, but that it has some unusual properties, all of which seem like they would be very useful in fighting a cold. But apparently there's also something special in it, some element or ingredient that they haven't been able to identify yet, and whatever it is, it appears to speed up the process, and kills a cold very quickly."

Adair nodded. He still hadn't said anything.

"I know I shouldn't have gone back down in the cave without you, but after I found out what this "stuff" is, or what it might be, I needed to get some more samples to take back to Los Angeles, and we were planning on going back to L. A. yesterday. I didn't want to bother you, and I thought one quick trip back to the room would be all right. Mr. Adair I wasn't going anywhere else or doing any exploring on my own. I just needed to get some more samples. Believe me, I learned a lesson. But at the same time, that rock slide could have happened even if you'd been with me, and they still would have had to dig us out."

"Yeah, I reckon that might be so, but from what Jennie said, you didn't tell her you were going down in there either, so I suppose you didn't tell no one."

"I guess you're right Mr. Adair, and I am sorry. I shouldn't have done it and I apologize. If you'll accept that, I'd like to talk to you about what I want to do with the cave, and where I'm going to need your help."

"I'm listenin', Mr. McCarthy."

"I'm going to take the samples I brought out yesterday back to Los Angeles to do some more testing. In the meantime, I don't want anyone going down in that cave. A lot of people know the cave is there now, and there's no one staying out on the farm to keep an eye on it."

"Not many folks around here would bother with it," Adair said.

"I'm sure that's true, Mr. Adair, but it only takes one. Or some kids could decide to go down in there. This is where I need your help. Jennie and I have to go back to Los Angeles tomorrow morning. The first thing I need to do is to get a locked gate or door or something on the entrance in the woods to the cave, and as soon as possible. Can you do that for me?

He nodded, "I reckon so."

"Great. I'd like for you to start on it tomorrow if you can. Also, if you have some idea as to how much you think that will cost, I'll leave a check with you, and then we'll settle up any difference when you're finished. I think the rock slide will take care of the other entrance."

He scribbled on a piece of paper for a couple of minutes and then gave me a number that was a lot less than I thought it would be.

"That ought to be right close."

"Does that include your time?" I asked.

"Yep. Includes me and any help I may need. If it ends up any different than that, I'll let you know."

"Great. It's a deal." As I said before, some things sure are a lot cheaper out in the country than they are in the big city.

"Now, I may need some additional samples of the "stuff" from time to time. When I do, I'd like for you to bring them out for me, and they'll need to be shipped in a container that will keep them at about the same temperature that they're in down in the cave. I'll figure out how to do that and let you know."

"I reckon we can do that."

"By the way, when I was trapped down in there I saw several rats. Do you have any idea how they got in the cave?"

"Couldn't say," Adair said. "I've seen 'em down in caves before a time or two. They's pack rats, generally. Sometimes they come in the same way we do. Other times I reckon they find some other way to get in. Could be they's two or three other places to get in that cave of yours, and it don't take much of a hole for a varmint like that to get in and out."

"That's something else I would like to have you think about. From a security point of view I'd like to have that cave explored to see if there are any other entrances. I'd like to have you do that, Mr. Adair, but if you don't want to do it, I'd appreciate it if you could find someone to do it for me who I can trust."

"Well, things is a mite slow around here this time of the year. I reckon I could find the time." I decided that Jim Adair could smell money just like anyone else.

"O.K.," I replied. "That would be terrific. I'd much rather work with you if you can do it, Mr. Adair. Let's start the exploration as soon as you can. You let me know how much I owe you at the end of every week, and I'll send you a check. Again, about those rats, are they dangerous? I was really concerned about what might have happened if I had been trapped down there for a couple of days."

"Can't say as I ever heard of 'em hurting anybody, but if they was hungry enough, no tellin' what they might do. I don't reckon I'd like to be down there with a bunch of starving rats if I was the only other thing around to eat."

That was kind of the way I felt about it.

I nodded, "Yeah."

Adair and I shook hands. I handed him a card with my office and home phone numbers on it. "I'll be staying in touch with you, Mr. Adair, but if anything comes up, call me at either number, any time. And again, I'm sorry for the trouble I caused everybody."

"Well, sir," he said. "I reckon you are."

Jennie and I were on the plane back to Los Angeles the next morning. After we got settled in on the plane and were up in the air we both ordered a Bloody Mary.

I held up the glass. "Well, Jennie, here's to McCarthy's Cave. It may turn out to be the ninth wonder of the world after all."

I pulled a yellow pad out of my briefcase, and starting putting down some figures. Thinking about it raised the possibility that we might be able to harvest two crops a year, not just one, which would raise the total crop from one million pieces a year to two million.

"What are you doing?" Jennie asked.

"I'm just playing around with numbers. I figure as a rough calculation that there ought to be about a million individual stalks of that 'stuff' down in the cave, maybe more than that the way it seems to grow back. Now, how much do you think a consumer would pay for one?"

"I don't have any idea," Jennie said, "but remember, it may take two of them. I ate two."

"I know. We'll have to find that out, but just take a guess."

"O.K. A dollar," she said.

"A dollar! Come on, get serious."

"O.K. A hundred dollars." She was pulling my leg.

"Very funny. But seriously, let's take a look at it. You catch a cold. If you're lucky you're just miserable for a week. If you're unlucky, you may have to go to a doctor. That's twenty to fifty dollars, depending. Then you may have to take time off work, buy cough drops, cough medicine, tissues, cold pills and vitamins. So a cold not only makes you feel lousy, but, one way or another, it can cost you a lot of money. Not only that, but you can pass it on to the rest of your family or the people you work with."

Jennie nodded, "Yeah, you're right."

"O.K., so what's it worth to avoid all of that? Also keep in mind that we have a limited supply of the "stuff". Five million stalks may not go very far in a country the size of the United States, much less the world. It does appear that it regenerates itself, but right now we don't know how fast that process is and if the new growth will have the same properties. And we have no idea of what the shelf life of the "stuff" would be. Will it last a couple of weeks, a couple of months, indefinitely? There are a lot of things we don't know."

"That's becoming obvious," Jennie said.

"All right. Let's say, just for the moment, that consumers would be willing to pay twenty-five dollars a dose. And let's say that our selling price to the drug stores would be ten or twelve dollars, just as a guess. The product is so unique that maybe we wouldn't have to give them any more, but to tell you the truth I don't know what kind of margin they make."

"To tell you the truth," Jennie said, "I think there's a lot you don't know about the drug business."

"Maybe," I said, sort of ignoring her remark, "but if we could net, bottom line, five dollars a stalk, that's five million dollars! Even after taxes that would leave three million or so. And suppose the "stuff" grows back in a year. That's three million a year!" My head was starting to spin as we talked about the numbers.

"Sounds good," she said, not sounding very enthusiastic. I knew something was bugging her.

"Yeah," I nodded, "I think getting this organized and on the market is going to be a full time job, Jennie. I'd have to set up a sales organization, arrange for distribution, and under a controlled temperature, which is probably more complicated." I shook my head. "It looks like you and Paul are going to have to run the agency while I concentrate on this business."

"I think you're getting in over your head," Jennie replied.

"Oh, I guess you don't think I could handle something like this. Nothing but a small time advertising guy." I was getting a little hot.

"Brian, I just think you're getting into a business that you don't know anything about."

"All right, then. Just what would you suggest?"

"Well, you could hire someone who has some experience with drugs to run this, or better yet, sell the "stuff" to a pharmaceutical company on a royalty or per piece basis, and let them worry about the marketing and distribution. Even if you got a dollar a piece, that's a million dollars Brian. That's more money than you ever thought you'd see in a lifetime."

"Yeah, I hear you, Jennie, but damn it, I've had this itch for a while to do something, to get involved in a business with a product that I control! I get a little tired of always being the outsider, the guy from the agency. And this "stuff" is a marketing man's dream. The possibilities for PR and advertising are unbelievable."

"I think I know how you feel, Brian, and I'm not trying to be a wet blanket, but it just seems like there are a lot of things to consider. I would presume that we'll have to get some kind of government approval on the "stuff", that it may require some kind of testing - I don't know - it just seems to be pretty complicated."

I nodded grudgingly, "Yeah, those are probably things we'll have to consider."

"Besides that, we don't even know what kinds of costs might be involved. It could be expensive."

I lapsed into silence. Thinking about problems that might arise, I was starting to realize the size and complexity of the undertaking. And all of this in an industry I didn't know a damned thing about in the first place. What she said made obvious good sense, but I was too stubborn to admit it at the moment.

The seat belt sign flashed on, and the stewardess's voice came on the intercom. We were back home. What a trip!

As we glided down toward the runway in the final flight pattern I said to Jennie, "Like you said, I suppose we will have to get some kind of government clearance or approval on this. What is it, the Food and Drug Agency, or something like that?" They say ignorance is bliss.

Chapter Twelve

No, McCarthy, you dummy! It is not the Food and Drug Agency. It is the Food and Drug Administration, the FDA., as I was to become painfully aware of.

I would guess that most of us have dealt with some kind of bureaucracy at one time or another, from someone at your local city hall to - God forbid - the IRS. But they all pale in comparison to the FDA, at least in my own personal experience, and maybe that was just me and the person I had to deal with.

The worst thing is that they know they can't be fired. They can make life absolutely miserable for you if they choose to, and they know it, and they know that you know it, and there isn't a hell of a lot the average person can do about it. The abuse of power.

Anyway, after Jennie and I got back to L. A. and we were settled back down in our routine, I began to make some discreet inquiries with a few people I know around town about the pharmaceutical business, and how it works. After a couple of conversations, in which people described the difficulties of dealing with the FDA, I was beginning to realize that I was a babe in the woods. It had become obvious, even to me, that I was going to have to get some professional help, so I got the name of a consultant, a Mr. J. Phillips Monroe, from a friend of mine who knew him, and who said he seemed to know his way around the drug business.

I called Monroe, and we chatted for a couple of minutes, but I told him I really didn't want to discuss the matter in any detail over the phone, so we arranged to meet at my office the following Tuesday.

Now my second pet peeve after bureaucrats are consultants. I'm sure you've heard the old gag about the definition of a consultant, someone who borrows your watch to tell you what time it is, and then keeps the watch. However, I must admit that there are times when consultants really are useful, like when you have a specific, temporary, problem in your business, and don't have anyone in the company who has experience or background in that area. Then you ought to go out and get some help. Obviously, in this case I needed help from someone with experience in the drug industry.

I also called Parker at Branson Blades early the next morning.

"Hello, Les. Brian here."

"Hi, Brian. "How're you doing?"

"O. K., I guess. I saw the article about you all in the Journal."

"Oh, yeah. We need to talk about that."

"I'd like to do that. When can we get together?"

"Well, I think I can clear lunch away today. How would that be?"

"Great. I'll pick you up at noon."

He was ready when I got there, and we walked down to a restaurant near his office. Branson Blades had been in the business of manufacturing cutting instruments of various kinds for over fifty years, but the current president, Phil Branson, grandson of the founder, had taken the business to a new plateau. We had been handling their advertising for about six years now, which consisted of periodic ads in several trade journals. We also took care of their collateral stuff, like brochures, price sheets and PR.

When we were seated, I looked across the table at Les, who was basically a nice guy.

"O. K., Les. Tell me what's going on."

He nodded. "All right, Brian. I'll give it to you straight. As you read in the paper, we're planning on taking the company public. Phil decided a couple of years ago that we should come up with a line of cutlery for consumers, and we've been developing a line of products. It's been pretty hush-hush."

"Yeah. Obviously."

"We know that it's going to take a lot of money to begin to build a brand name, you know, advertising, promotion, all of that stuff, and that's the reason for the public offering."

"Well, that's pretty exciting news, Les, and we'd like to be a part of that. I hope it's in the cards."

Les grimaced, and rubbed his forehead with his hand, "I told you I'd be straight with you, Brian. I don't think it is in the cards."

"Why not? We've been doing a good job for you all for several years now. At least I haven't had any complaints."

"Yes, you have done a good job, Brian, and we appreciate it, but frankly, Phil feels that we need a bigger shop for this. One that's done a lot of consumer advertising."

"How do you feel about it?"

"How do I feel? Well, first of all, I don't get to vote on this one. Phil's already made up his mind, but secondly, I guess I'd have to agree with him."

"Are you talking to anyone yet?"

"No, not directly, but we've been making some inquiries."

"Are you going to go into a review?"

"Probably."

"What's our chances of being part of that. We've invested a lot of time in Branson, and we'd at least like to have a shot at it."

"I don't know, Brian, but I'll tell you what. I'll talk it over with Phil and see how he feels about it, but very honestly, I don't the chances are real good. He's been pretty vocal about this."

Brian shook his head. "Jesus. This comes as a real blow, Les. Branson is a pretty big part of our business."

"I know it is, Brian, and I feel lousy about it, but it's pretty well out of my hands."

"What's the timetable?"

"Well, we want to have the product in the market by this fall, which means that we need to introduce the product line early summer. Actually, we're a little behind schedule now, and we'll have to move fast. We'll probably start the agency review process in a week or so."

"So we stay on until a new agency takes over?"

"Oh, sure."

"Well, we'd still like to be included in the review."

"I understand, Brian, and I'll get you an answer on that as soon as I can."

"I'd appreciate that, Les. I'm just kind of sorry I had to read about this in the paper." It was a dumb thing to say, but I just couldn't help myself.

"I'm sorry about that, too."

I got my answer the next day. It was no, and I called in Paul and Jennie. They already know about my lunch conversation.

"Well, gang, I just talked to Les, and it's no deal. We will not be part of the review."

"You're kidding," Paul said. "That stinks."

"Yeah, I guess so, but that's life in the advertising business."

"What to we do now?" Paul asked.

"Good question." Actually Jennie and I had talked about it at great length the night before. "First thing is that we're going to have to sit down and take a good hard look at the books. Obviously some people may have to go. A good part of the problem is that we don't have any new business working right now, which is probably my fault. But there's something else that we should talk about, Paul."

We had not told him as yet about the cave and the "stuff", and it was time to do that, and I took him through the whole story, including showing him samples, which were now stored in a small refrigerator in the corner of my office. When I finished, Paul shook his head.

"This is difficult to comprehend, Brian."

"Yeah, I know what you mean, Paul, but I suspect that there's a long road ahead of us, a long, rocky road."

"What are you going to do?"

"Well, first thing, I've got a so-called expert coming in here next Tuesday, and I'm going to talk to him, and then we'll take it from there. I'll keep you plugged in. And let's keep the news about Branson quiet until we decide what needs to be done, O. K.?"

***

J. Phillips Monroe showed up promptly at my office on Tuesday morning at nine o'clock. He was another person right out of central casting. Monroe looked to be in his mid-forties, and was about medium height and weight. He was dressed in a dark blue three-piece suit with a modestly striped tie, and was carrying a brief case, and was sporting a short beard and mustache, very neatly trimmed.

"Mr. McCarthy? J. Philips Monroe." He had a very firm, very businesslike handshake, and one of those deep, resonant voices that reverberated throughout the room.

"Mr. Monroe, it's nice to meet you. This is my assistant, Jennie Carson. She's going to join us for the meeting. And this is Charlie the Dog"

"How do you do." He said and shook hands with Jennie, and I saw her wince. It was still very firm. He looked down at Charlie with something very close to distaste. Obviously not a dog lover, but then I didn't think Charlie was crazy about consultants.

"How can I be of assistance to you, Mr. McCarthy?"

"Well, Mr. Monroe, we seemed to have stumbled upon a very unusual property, but before we can really discuss the product, I'd like for you to sign a confidentiality agreement." I handed him a copy of the agreement I'd had prepared, a fairly standard document.

He looked it over carefully, and then nodded. "Yes, that seems to be in order." He took out a pen and signed it on the appropriate line, and handed it back to me. "I'd appreciate a copy of that."

"Of course. We'll get you one before you leave." I signed on the line below his signature.

This guy was great at consulting, a natural. He quickly established from the outset that the tone of this discussion was going to *very serious*. "Tell me what you have in mind, Mr. McCarthy."

"I will make it as brief as I can, Mr. Monroe. I recently inherited a small farm in Kentucky, and while inspecting the property, I discovered a cave on the property. I was exploring it with a couple of professional spelunkers," I thought this would be the proper word to use with J. P. Monroe, "when I discovered a very unusual substance growing down in the cave."

"I see," he said, raising his eyebrows, and looking rather dubious.

"It so happened that Miss Carson, who was with me, was in the midst of a very bad cold. However, she consumed a small amount of this substance, sort of by accident, really, and her cold cleared up completely overnight. Just like that"

"That's right," Jennie said. "I should have been fighting that cold for at least another week. It was just getting started."

"I'll show you what the substance looks like," I said.

I took a piece out of the refrigerator, and put it down on the table in front of him. The "stuff" - we were going to have to get a better name for it - seemed to be holding up nicely, which really made sense when you think about it. It may very well have been growing down in the cave for years or even hundreds of years at that temperature.

"Very interesting," he remarked, not very convincingly, and J. P. was looking at me at first like I was some kind of certified California weirdo. I think he was dying to ask me, at one point, if this was some kind of practical joke, April Fool's Day, or something, but couldn't quite bring himself to ask the question. In a way I could understand how he felt. Some guy you've never met before pulls some vegetation out of a canister and tells you he found it in a cave, and that it is an overnight cure for the common cold.

Finally he frowned and stood up. "I don't really think this is something I could help you with."

I nodded. "I know what you're thinking Mr. Monroe, that I am some kind of a crackpot. But before you leave, take a look at this lab report. I had this substance analyzed by a laboratory in Louisville while we were at the farm."

He looked over the report, and you could see his attitude changing.

"Mr. Monroe, I would like to have some further testing done here in L. A. Can you recommend someone?"

"Yes, Encino Labs would be excellent for this kind of project."

"Fine. Let's get it tested again, and then see how you feel about it."

"That's an excellent idea, although I am somewhat reassured by this report." He waved the papers at me. He must have decided that we were serious about this, because he delivered a five minute dissertation on the difficulties of dealing with the FDA, and the various kinds of booby traps and quicksand that lay ahead, which were alluded to but not quite spelled out in detail. The bottom line of all of this was that it was important for us to understand that we had done the best possible thing. We had called in J. Phillips Monroe, who would guide us through this governmental maze.

"Could you tell us on what financial basis you normally work with your clientele?" I asked. Now I was starting to talk like a consultant.

"Certainly," he replied, accompanied by a rather oily smile. "Our usual arrangement is twelve hundred dollars per diem, plus expenses. We do not bill in increments of less than a half a day, even if an hour or two is involved, the reason being of course is that it precludes us from meeting with other clients, and so for all intents and purposes the remainder of that half day is lost to me as productive time."

I made a quick mental calculation. If this guy worked forty weeks a year, five days a week, he would earn $240,000. Since he probably worked out of his house, or had one of those low cost executive suites, chances are he had little or no overhead. Not bad. Oh yes, any expenses that he incurred on a client's behalf, such as travel, entertainment, phone charges and whatever, would be billed separately and in addition to his per diem fee.

"Perhaps you could be a little more specific about just what it is that you will do for us, Mr. Monroe."

He smiled again. "Mr. McCarthy, you are about to venture into waters that I believe for you are uncharted. It would be much like my deciding to enter the world of advertising, one of which I know very little, particularly from the agency side. The drug industry in quite complex, and in addition to that you are going to be dealing with an extremely bureaucratic organization, the FDA." He raised his hand. "Please understand that I do not offer that as a criticism of the FDA, but they have evolved a complex structure and approach to licensing new products. They feel, and I concur with them, that they are the guardians, to a large degree, of the health and welfare of the citizens of this country, and they take that responsibility very seriously."

I damn near stood up and saluted.

"Our mission," he continued, "since we do know these waters quite well, is to save you time and money in getting your product to market. Without that kind of guidance you could find yourself making many false starts, which would be expensive, both in terms of adding months to the process and increasing your costs substantially. We will be well worth the fees we are paid."

"I think it would be helpful to me if you were to put some of this down on paper for me, without the meter running, " I added. "In the meantime, I will contact Encino Labs and get some additional testing done. Why don't we get back together on Thursday morning."

"Nine o'clock?"

"That would be fine. And by the way, Mr. Monroe, I am very serious about the confidentiality of this project."

He looked at me like I had insulted his entire ancestry. "Mr. McCarthy, if I mentioned this to anyone, it would a breech of ethics!"

"Nothing personal, Mr. Monroe. Just making a point. I'll see you on Thursday."

I called Encino Labs, and set up an appointment to go out that afternoon. The technician I met with was named Phil Summers, and he was pale and skinny, kind of like the guy at the lab in Louisville, but no acne. The routine was pretty much the same as it had been at Reynolds Labs, except that Encino charged $500 an hour and their receptionist was flat chested. I told them to do some basic testing, and that if any additional work might be necessary we could discuss that later. I gave Phil a brief description of where we had found the "stuff", but that was all. He agreed to call me back the next morning with a preliminary report.

He called the next morning about ten and told me, almost verbatim, what I had been told by Reynolds Labs, including the fact that, once again, there was this strange substance that they had not been able to identify in their initial analysis. I asked him to give me an estimate on how much it would cost for further testing on the mysterious element, and he said he would call me back. So far they were into me for fifteen hundred bucks. I asked him to fax over a copy of the report.

J. P. returned on Thursday, and Jennie joined us. I wanted her take on all of this.

"I took some samples out to Encino Labs, Mr. Monroe. Here's a copy of their report."

He read it over. "Very much like the one you obtained in Louisville."

"Yes it is. Feel free to call Phil Summers if you like."

"I will certainly do that, Mr. McCarthy, once we have established some kind of relationship."

Very cool, Monroe, I thought.

He then pulled a two-page document out of his brief case, which he handed to me to read.

The bottom line was that our medical discovery was going to have to go through an approval process with the FDA, and because it would probably be viewed as new and untested, it was likely that the administrative process would be quite lengthy and quite expensive.

"Just what do you mean by quite lengthy and quite expensive, Mr. Monroe?" I asked.

"Well, Mr. McCarthy, first of all, some additional testing of the substance will undoubtedly be required. The preliminary reports indicate that there is some ingredient that has yet to be identified. Even though the substance overall has apparently been found to be harmless, the *administration* - this was pronounced in a rather hollowed tone - "will undoubtedly want to ascertain exactly the nature and composition of all ingredients in the substance. They simply would not allow it to be released on the market until they are fully satisfied."

I nodded. "Yeah, I can understand that."

He continued. "Once that requirement has been satisfied they will want the substance to be tested with patients, under very controlled procedures, of course."

"Of course. How do we do that?"

"By having the testing conducted by an approved clinic. There are several here in Southern California that I am familiar with. I might add that the administration is familiar with them as well, which is quite important."

"I see. About how many people would we have to test?"

"Well, of course we would have to negotiate that with the administration, and it might depend to some extent on how the early testing is proceeding, and how favorable the results are with the early patients, but it could possibly involve as many as two or three hundred subjects."

"Hm." I looked at Jennie. "I'm beginning to get the idea. Can you give me some estimate of what we are talking about in terms of time and money?"

Monroe scribbled in a small notebook that had magically appeared from his coat pocket. "Please understand that this is only a preliminary estimate, and there are many factors to consider before arriving at a more exact number, but it could involve as much as two years, and perhaps two hundred and fifty to three hundred thousand dollars." He smiled. "Plus, of course, my fees."

I smiled weakly. "Of course." I got this sinking feeling in the pit of my stomach, mostly because I didn't have three hundred thousand dollars, and didn't know where to get it, even if I re-financed the house, which I really hated to consider. The equity I had in the house was my ace in the hole, my security blanket, and I didn't want to screw around with it unless I absolutely had to, especially with the Branson Blade situation looming ahead.

I looked at Jennie and then back at Monroe. "This is pretty serious stuff, Mr. Monroe. Is there any possible way we might be able to cut this procedure down? Frankly, that's a hell of a lot of money, and more than I could personally put into this project."

Monroe tilted his head, frowned and then nodded slowly. "We may be able to effect some reduction in the total expenditure, particularly through some of my contacts, but I wanted you to have a macro view on what a worst case scenario might be, particularly if you proceeded by yourself, without some expert knowledge of the administration and their procedures and regulations."

I digested all of this, and then said, "I'll tell you what, Mr. Monroe. Both Jennie and I believe in this product, and I just feel like we have to proceed on down the road, at least a little further, until we can get a better fix on all of this. But money is a problem. Unless of course we bring in some other people, which I haven't even considered at this point. I'm willing to hire you, but here's the deal. I'll pay you by the hour, not the day, at a rate of one hundred dollars an hour. I'll write you a check right now for one thousand dollars. That's ten hours."

Monroe nodded slightly, indicating simply an understanding of what I was saying, not agreement.

I continued. "What I want in return is a recommendation from you as to how we should proceed from here, with whom, doing what. At the end of that time, when the ten hours are used up, we'll sit down and decide what kind of future arrangement is mutually agreeable. However, if one hour of your time is going to cost me four because of scheduling or commuting, then we don't have a deal. You'll have to figure out some way to work around the schedule."

Monroe was probably a very good poker player. He sat and thought this over for a minute or so without changing expression. Finally he said, "Well, Mr. McCarthy, I don't ordinarily enter into this type of arrangement, but I must say that I am intrigued by your project and this remarkable substance. If it is really what you and Miss Carson believe it to be, it could have quite an impact on the industry, and I'd like to be associated with that, so let's proceed on that basis. And since we're going to be working together, why don't you call me J. P."

"O.K., J. P., and call me Brian." We shook hands. "What do we do first, J. P.?"

"Well, I believe the best way to proceed would be by meeting with some of the executive staff from the administration, getting some initial reaction and guidance from them, and then taking the appropriate action at that point. "

"I want to sit in on that meeting," I said.

He frowned. "Perhaps it might be best if I had a preliminary discussion with them before we bring you in. Some times I find that it is disconcerting to clients to discover how difficult and arbitrary the administration can be, particularly with individuals they are not already familiar with. On the other hand, if I were to go in and pave the way, so to speak, then you might find that your first meeting with the administration might sail along on calmer seas."

What a cliche! I shook my head emphatically. "Let's establish what our relationship is going to be, J. P. You are the navigator we have hired to guide our ship safely through these uncharted waters into the harbor, but I am the captain of the ship." I glanced out of the corner of my eye over at Jennie, who rolled her eyes up. I can cliche with the best of them. "It will be important for me to attend these kinds of meetings, so that I can begin to get a better feel for the industry, how it works, and just what the FDA is going to require."

J. P. obviously didn't like my response, but he finally agreed to it, and said he would call me as soon as a meeting could be set up.

"Who will this meeting be with?" I inquired.

"Most probably it will be with a Mr. Arnold Decker. He is a regional administrator here in Los Angeles."

I told him that would be fine, but first I wanted his recommendation as to how we should proceed. Maybe we didn't want to meet with the FDA.

We shook hands and J. Phillips Monroe departed. As soon as he was out the door and presumably out of earshot, Jennie erupted into laughter. "The captain of the ship! My God, that's wonderful," she said. "Captain McCarthy."

I was laughing too. "Listen, Jennie. When you're dealing with consultants you have to keep the dialogue on a very high plain. Seriously, though, what did you think of Monroe?" I had found that Jennie was a very good judge of character, and usually got a more accurate fix on people than I did.

She lowered her voice, mimicking Monroe. "It is my considered opinion that in the long term his services may prove to be satisfactory." We both laughed. She continued, "I guess he's O.K., Brian. He comes across as a little stuffy, but he may just naturally be that way. I suppose the worst thing that can happen is that you're going to be out a grand. I think we'll find out pretty fast whether he can deliver or not."

I nodded. "His resume looks pretty good. He was involved with product development and marketing with a couple of major drug firms. At least I recognized the names of the companies he was with, so he obviously does have a fair amount of industry experience."

"You think his estimates on costs are going to be realistic?" she asked.

"I don't have the foggiest idea, Jennie, but I have a hunch they may have been somewhat inflated so that he can show us later on how much money he can save us. I guess it'll pretty much depend on what we hear from the *administration*'," I said, imitating J. P.'s pronunciation of the word. "That should be an interesting meeting. I hear they can be pretty tough, at least according to a couple of people I've talked to."

The phone rang, and our receptionist buzzed in. "There's a Mr. Jim Adair on the line for you, Brian."

"Put him through," I said.

"Hello, Mr. Adair? How are things down in Kentucky?" I asked.

"Just fine, Mr. McCarthy. Thought I'd give you a call and tell you what was going on down here."

"Great. Listen, as long as we're going to be working together, why don't we make it Jim and Brian."

"All right, Mr. Mc - er Brian. Just wanted you to know we got a door up on the entrance to the cave back in the woods, and we padlocked it, so I reckon that ought to keep folks out. Actually, what we did was to put an iron gate across the opening. It's anchored into the rock on both sides and padlocked, so it's pretty secure. The other entrance is pretty well blocked by the rock-slide. However, the costs come out a little bit higher than I estimated, so I'll send you the charges."

"That's fine, Jim. Keep track of your phone bills, too, or any other expenses you have."

"I'll do that, Mr. Mc - Brian." It was obviously hard for Jim Adair to get on a first name basis with people he didn't know all that well. "Will and me'll probably go down in there next week and start pokin' around, see if they's anythin' else we can find down there. Also we'll see if they's any other way to get in or out of the cave."

"O.K., Jim. I'm sending you down a small refrigerated unit to ship samples back when I need them. It's battery powered, so you'll be able to send it by Mail Express or U.P.S."

"You want us to bring some out?"

"No, not yet. I'll let you know when I need some of the "stuff" back here."

"All right, Brian. By the way, I don't believe I mentioned this to you, but we had a pretty big earthquake down here around a year or so ago. That might be where that crack in the cave come from."

"Thanks Jim. That's interesting. You have many earthquakes in that area?"

"Nope. That was the first one in quite some time."

I felt a lot better with Jim Adair down at the other end. He was that kind of rock-solid guy you knew you could depend on, and I had the feeling that things in Kentucky were under control. At least they were for now.

Chapter Thirteen

J. P. Monroe called me back the next day, and said that we had a meeting set up for the following Tuesday at ten o'clock with Arnold Decker at the FDA. Giving J. P. the benefit of the doubt, I decided that he must have a certain amount of clout to get a meeting set up that quickly. He told me to bring the two lab reports along, but not to bring samples of the "stuff".

I showed up a little before ten at the FDA office. I told the receptionist who I was and who my appointment was with, but I suggested that she wait until Mr. Monroe arrived to call Mr. Decker. She informed me that Mr. Monroe had already arrived, and was inside with Mr. Decker, which I found interesting and a little annoying. I had told him I wanted to be present for any discussions.

Shortly after ten Monroe came through the door next to the receptionist's desk. We shook hands.

"Good morning, Brian. I arrived here a trifle early, and took the opportunity to chat a bit with Arnold." Yeah, sure you did, I thought. "Why don't we go on in," he said.

"I thought I made it plain to you that I wanted to be included in all discussions."

"So far, Mr. McCarthy, the discussions have been purely social."

We went through the door past an open area with several people working at whatever they were working at, and into an office. All the desks, chairs, file cabinets and furniture looked like the standard GSA stuff I remembered from my brief service career. Nothing fancy.

The man sitting behind the desk stood up, didn't smile, didn't offer to shake hands. "Mr. McCarthy? I'm Arnold Decker," he said, in a high, thin nasal voice.

He was tall, about six feet I'd say, and was rather gaunt and somber looking. He was fiftyish, with greying hair, combed straight back and thinning a bit. He was wearing wire-rimmed glasses that had a tendency to slip down on his nose, and his suit went out of style right after hula-hoops. The overall effect was the sort of caricature you might associate with an undertaker. He reminded me of an actor who played a lot of bit parts in the movies but whose name escapes me.

"Brian McCarthy, Mr. Decker. Nice to meet you." I suppose I shouldn't admit it, but I took an instant dislike to this guy, and before long I got the impression that the feeling was mutual. Sometimes the chemistry between two people can be instantly bad, which I guess was the case here.

"J. P. here has been telling me that you have come up with some strange kind of vegetation that you think has some unique properties. Perhaps you can tell me a little bit about it."

I wasn't thrilled with the word "strange", but launched into a fairly brief description of the recent events in Kentucky, including only those details that I thought were pertinent to our discussion.

Decker listened in silence, without comment or question, nervously tapping the desk with the end of a pencil, sometimes staring at the ceiling. When I had finished, he peered at me over his glasses, cleared his throat, shook his head, and said, "This is all most unusual." It was not the greatest display of enthusiasm I had ever witnessed.

"Yes. I suppose it is. As perhaps J. P. has told you, I am not from the pharmaceutical industry, Mr. Decker. I am in the advertising business. But if this substance can really cure the common cold as quickly as it appears to, it would seem to be a great thing for our society."

"Possibly so, Mr. McCarthy." He wasn't giving me any slack. "However, this is what we would almost certainly classify as a new product, and consequently, there would have to be a long trail of testing and procedures before it could ever be approved for public consumption."

"I think I understand that in general," I said. "Perhaps you could be more specific in detail as to just what has to be done."

The question seemed to annoy him, and he got a little testy, his voice getting higher, almost whiny. "Well, Mr. McCarthy. Let's start with first things first," he said rather impatiently. "The initial requirement would be to thoroughly test this substance, to make sure that it does not contain any ingredients that might be harmful to people."

"We have a preliminary report from a lab down in Louisville. This certainly appears to be favorable." I laid the report on the table in front of him.

"Yes, I'd like to look through this. That would be a first step. Then we can determine what further testing might be required. Let me read through it, and I'll get back to you. Is this a copy I can keep?"

"Yes it is," I said, forcing a smile. I definitely had the feeling now that Arnold Decker and I would not be taking any family vacations together.

He tapped his fingers on the report I had given him. "I am sure that this lab down in Kentucky is reliable, but I would be more comfortable if it was from one of our labs here in Southern California, one that I am familiar with."

J.P. chimed in, "We'll consider that, Arnold."

"When do you think we can get back together?" I asked.

"Why don't you call me, or better yet, have J. P. call me in a month or two." Arnold said.

"A month or two?" My eyebrows shot up involuntarily. J. P. was trying to give me eye signals.

"We're very busy here, Mr. McCarthy, and quite candidly, are understaffed. This may come as a surprise to you, but we are not given unlimited funds by the government, and I was not just sitting here, hoping that you would come in and help fill up my day. Now, as an observation, I realize that all of this is very new to you, and frankly, you might be better off just to leave this sort of thing to professionals." Sounded like a commercial for J. P. Monroe to me. "I'm sure you're very good at advertising things," this was said with a verbal sneer, "but we have a whole different situation here. This is serious business. And I would really like another lab report." He stood up, indicating that the interview was over.

I've been insulted by experts, but this guy was one of the best. I thought I had controlled my temper rather admirably, although I could feel my face was starting to flush. "I'll consider what you've said, Mr. Decker, although it certainly would be helpful to me to understand a little more about your procedures."

"I suppose it might. Where is this substance located?"

"Somewhere in the Middle West." I didn't want to be more specific than that.

He stuck out his hand. His handshake was clammy, weak. and just what I had expected. "I see. Well, it was nice to meet you, Mr. McCartney."

"McCarthy," I corrected him. "Nice to meet you, Mr. Decker."

I walked out of his office with J. P. right behind. When we got out of the lobby I turned to him. "Charming friends you have, J. P."

J. P. shrugged. "Don't misjudge him, Brian. It's simply a matter of getting to know him. I've had a relationship with Decker for years now, and I am confident I know the best way to handle him. I also believe that I can move that month schedule up somewhat. Let me call him, and I'll get back to you."

"O.K., J. P. I'll leave it in your hands. But Decker could go through that report in fifteen minutes. It's ridiculous to tell us a month or two."

"Let's see what happens, Brian."

"Do you suppose he's still pissed off because he flunked the Dale Carnegie course?"

J. P. didn't smile. "Please, Brian, just leave it to me."

Somehow I had the feeling that much of this meeting had been staged for my benefit, but I sure as hell couldn't prove it. Anyway, after the first inning it was FDA 1, McCarthy O.

I thought about the meeting all the way back to the office. Jennie came into my office right after I got back. "How did it go?" she asked.

I shrugged, still fuming. "It wasn't the warmest meeting I've ever had in my life." I filled her in on the details. "This whole drug business, it makes me feel like I'm in a foreign country or something. Maybe we'd better have Jan do some background on pharmaceutical companies for me, stuff like their sales in the cold remedy business, share of market, you know, whatever she can dig up quickly in the next couple of days."

Jan Thompson was our research staff, among other things.

"Are you going to talk to some of them?" Jennie asked.

"Well, I'm starting to think about it, Jennie. But it still may be that we'll have to do some initial testing ourselves before any of them would take us seriously. I just think that we're going to have to establish the fact, at least to some extent, that this is a legitimate and effective product before anyone will think we're for real."

"I wish you would really think about turning it over to someone else, Brian. I have this feeling that we're getting in over our heads. And right now, the agency needs you. You're the main contact with most of our clients, and you know that, just as well as I do. You also know just how important personal relationships are to the business. Whether you want to admit it or not Brian, you're the key to the success of this Agency."

"Yeah, like the Branson account?"

"Come on. There wasn't anything you could do about that."

"Well, you may be right, Jennie, and I've pretty well given up on the idea of starting our own company, but I'd like to play it out a little longer, and see what happens."

J. P. called a couple of days later and told me, as I had expected, that he had been able to move Decker's schedule up, and that we would get back together in about ten days. He also told me I should arrange some way to take a couple of samples down to the meeting with me, under refrigeration, and that he would call back with the exact time of the meeting.

In the meantime, Jan Thompson brought me in the information I'd asked for on the pharmaceutical companies. There were quite a number of companies that supplied cold remedy products of one kind or another, but two of them dominated the business, with about an equal share of market, close to twenty percent each. They were Koldex Corporation and Belmont Pharmaceuticals, Inc. The difference was that cold remedy products comprised virtually all of Koldex's sales, whereas Belmont was much more diversified, and overall was a lot bigger company. The rest of the market was pretty well split up among a number of other companies.

I called Jan Thompson on the intercom and asked her to stop by. When she came in I pointed at her report. "That's good stuff, Jan. Thank you. What I'd like you to do is dig a little deeper on two of these companies, Koldex and Belmont. I need all of the background material that's reasonably available, information on the company, on the management, whatever you can find. I don't want you to spend a ton of time on this, so let's see what pops out from the newspapers and trade magazines, O.K.?"

"Sure. What's the priority?"

"No huge rush, Jan. Sometime in the next week would be fine."

"Are we going after a drug client?"

"Well, it's possible." Jennie and I had decided to keep the news about the "stuff" quiet around the office, and had told no one about the events in Kentucky except for Paul Miller. Nothing had been said yet about Branson.

Charlie, in addition to being a fine pet, was also kind of a guard dog. If anyone came near the house, he would bark his head off, and he did that night. I went outside and looked around but did not see anyone or anything, but knowing Charlie, there was something out there, But I did hear a car start up out in the street. I watched it drive by but couldn't see the driver.

I went back inside and petted Charlie on his head. "Good boy, Charlie. You keep an eye on things for us." He wagged his tail with enthusiasm and disappeared back into our bedroom where we kept his cage, his nighttime sleeping place.

"You know", I said to Jennie, I wish I could teach that dog something useful."

"Like what?" she asked.

"I don't know. Maybe like going out to get the newspaper in the morning."

"Why don't you teach him something really useful."

"Like what?"

"Maybe like playing the piano or the accordion. He could be on TV. Make a lot of money. Be famous."

"Very funny."

Jennie, Paul and I got together the next day to discuss the events so far. We decided to create a company, at least on paper, and keep moving forward on the project until the next meeting with the FDA. We called the company McCarthy Pharmaceutical, which was certainly catchy, and we finally came up with a name for the stuff. It was Jennie's idea, and I kind of liked it, at least in the interim. Cavernite. It had sort of a ring to it.

The next meeting with Mr. Warmth down at the FDA took place on a Tuesday, just two weeks after our first encounter, and after we had received a lab report from Encino Labs. It was very much like the one done in Louisville, and J. P. had taken a copy down to Decker. I decided it would be best for me to try to be as amiable and agreeable as possible. J. P. Monroe was there, of course, working on his ten hours. We all shook hands and sat down around Decker's desk.

"First of all, Mr. Decker, I appreciate your looking at the lab reports so quickly. What do you think?"

"Well, Mr. McCarthy, I'm not familiar with this laboratory in Louisville, but I do know the people at Encino. I would say that the reports are somewhat encouraging. However, what concerns me most is this element or ingredient that neither one of them was able to identify. Obviously some major investigation and analysis is going to have to be done here. We have to know exactly what this element is before we can proceed with any kind of patient testing."

I nodded in agreement. "I understand that, Mr. Decker. Any suggestions as to how we should proceed, or who should do the work?"

J. P. interrupted here. "I gave Mr. McCarthy the names of three laboratories, Arnold, all of which are on your approved list."

"Any of those would do, Mr. McCarthy, and it might be best to get a couple of opinions. Of course, you could select another lab that's not on the list if you wish, but we should discuss that ahead of time to make sure that they are reliable and that we are familiar with their work."

"Those three are fine with me," I replied.

Decker looked at the small, refrigerated box I was carrying. "You brought some samples of the, er substance?"

"Yes. We have a name for it, at least an interim name for it for convenience sake. Cavernite."

"Cavernite." Decker glanced at J. P. "I see." I could tell he was not terribly impressed with the name. On the other hand, I wasn't sure just what would impress Decker.

I opened up the door, took a sample out and placed it on the desk in front of him. He grimaced and picked it up gingerly, as though it might be poisonous or had just crawled out from under a rock. He scrutinized it rather carefully, sniffed at it, and laid it back down on the desk. I quickly put the sample back in the box, deciding that it would be best to get it out of his sight.

"I must confess that I have never seen anything quite like that before, Mr. McCarthy," Decker said. "Very curious. Well, let's proceed on with the testing and we'll see what happens next."

I couldn't let it alone. "Do you think we're making any progress, Mr. Decker?"

"Progress? Progress?" He shook his head. "I don't believe I could really answer that question, Mr. McCarthy. We see a lot of products come through here, and I must confess that this appears to be one of the strangest I've ever seen. Some of those products never see the light of day, and I wouldn't be surprised if yours wasn't one of those."

My Irish temper flared up. I just couldn't help myself. "I'm a little surprised to hear you say that, Mr. Decker, considering that we've just begun testing. I hope Cavernite gets a fair shot."

We were both glaring at each other now. "Are you intimating that we would treat a product unfairly here, Mr. McCarthy?"

"I'm not intimating anything, Mr. Decker. I really don't know how you operate here, but it sounded to me a minute ago as though you were pre-judging this product. I hope that's not the case, because if it is, we would be wasting our time and money to go through this testing procedure."

"You may very well be wasting your time and money anyway, Mr. McCarthy. There are no guarantees here. You'll just have to take your chances."

"Thank you. I'll do that." I headed for the door.

J. P. jumped up. "I'll be with you in just a minute, Brian. Would you mind waiting outside for me?"

"Sure." I left the two of them standing there. About five minutes later J. P. came out of the door. He did not have a very happy look on his face.

"Brian, I really wish you hadn't taken that tone with him. Frankly, it's making the situation with Decker rather difficult."

I grimaced, "Yeah, I know, J. P. I should have kept my cool. I guess there's something about Decker that rubs me the wrong way."

"I know that I don't need to point this out to you, Brian, but the fact is that we need Decker a lot more than he needs us."

"I really can't argue with that logic." I thought for a moment. "Maybe I should discuss this situation with a Congressman I've done some work for."

J. P. frowned. "You might wish to think that course of action over carefully, Brian. That could very well be more negative than positive by causing further irritation with Decker."

"Yeah, it might. On the other hand, I want Decker to know that if we don't feel like we're getting a fair shot on this that we do have somebody we can talk to. You and I both know he shouldn't have made that statement in there. Maybe the best thing is for me to stay away from Decker as much as possible and let you handle him."

J. P. nodded a vigorous agreement. "Frankly, I think that might be a very prudent course of action."

"In the meantime, let's keep moving this along. Why don't you talk to Summers at Encino Lab, explain to him what kind of testing we are going to need, and have him give either you or me an estimate before he proceeds."

After they left The FDA office, Decker's secretary Betty Allbright walked in his office.

"What was that all about?" she inquired.

"Just a couple of guys with a crazy idea," he said. "But just in case, you had better start a file on them. Here are a couple of lab reports for the file." He handed her the two reports.

When Decker left for lunch, she got the two reports out of her desk drawer and glanced through them. Then she got out a small address book, looked up Hugo Gunderson's private phone number and dialed it.

He answered on the second ring.

"Gunderson here."

"Mr. Gunderson. Betty Allbright at the FDA. I think I have something you might be interested in."

"Really?"

"Yes. There were a couple of men in here this morning to see Mr. Decker."

"Yes?"

"They appear to have discovered some kind of vegetation that is an overnight cure for the cold."

"I see."

"They left copies of two lab reports on this substance."

"Can you make me copies?"

"Yes, I can."

Gunderson thought for a moment.

"Suppose I have a Mr. Moretti pick them up this afternoon."

"That would be fine. I'll have them ready. Tell him to ask the receptionist for me."

"I will. And he will have something for you." He hung up the phone and buzzed his secretary. "Have Mr. Moretti come see me."

"When"?

"Now."

Gino Moretti grew up in a poor section of Brooklyn, the only child of a single mother, who had only two interests in life: booze and boy friends. As a result Gino pretty much raised himself. It was a tough part of town so Gino grew up as a tough kid.

When he was eighteen his mother passed away, from a combination of things, really, and tired of the New York weather, he moved to Los Angeles. Shortly after moving there he was hired by Hugo Gunderson, who had quickly read his character. His job was to do the things that Hugo didn't want anyone else to know about, and he did that very well.

While Gunderson was waiting for Moretti, he hung up the phone, and dialed the combination number for his private safe in the bottom drawer of his desk. When it opened he took five one hundred dollar bills out of it, put them in an envelope, sealed it and wrote "Betty Allbright" on the outside. There was a knock on his door and Gino Moretti walked in.

"You wanted to see me, boss?"

"I want you to go over to the FDA Office this afternoon. When you get there ask for Miss Allbright. Don't talk to anyone else. She will give you a package to bring back to me, then hand her this envelope."

***

J. P. called me the next afternoon. "Summers tells me that to break that element down and thoroughly identify and analyze it, he estimates will be in the neighborhood of about twenty-five thousand dollars. And they will require additional samples, about a dozen."

"Some neighborhood. The samples are no problem, J. P., it's the money. This is starting to add up. I presume that when he uses the word "estimates" that it is possible it could go higher?"

"I presume so," J. P. said.

"I'll have to get back to you." I decided that maybe it would be a good idea if I called Summers myself.

To quote Senator Everett Dirksen's famous remark, "A billion here and a billion there, and pretty soon you're talking real money." We weren't in the billions, but with the two lab reports so far, the fee to J. P., the cost of putting the door on the cave, and now the further testing, we were in the sixty - seventy thousand dollar range, and just starting. The fact was, I just didn't have that kind of cash lying around, and if I started trying to bleed money out of the agency, I was going to create a whole other set of problems. There wasn't much blood there, anyway.

I sat down again with Paul and Jennie and went over the costs so far.

"Folks, we're beginning to look at a lot of money on this project," I started. "With the two lab tests, the money we're paying Monroe, the door we put on the cave for security, and now the full test the FDA is asking for, we're probably over seventy grand. Also the FDA is strongly suggesting that we have a second lab conduct a test as well, so that's probably another twenty-five thousand. Then we have to figure on some patient testing. I don't even have a cost on that, but if we started with twenty-five patients we could be looking at another fifty K."

Paul whistled. "Boy, it is starting to add up. Are there any alternatives?"

"We might be able to eliminate the second test, but I think this guy Decker from the FDA is down on us anyway, which is probably my fault, so I don't want to give him any excuses or reasons to object to the product if I can possibly avoid it."

"Couldn't we approach a couple of the drug companies now, before we spend all this money for testing?" Jennie asked.

"Yeah, I suppose we could, Jennie. The problem is that without some significant backup in testing, some validity for Cavernite, they may not take us very seriously. And, if we take it a little further down the road we may be able to make a better deal with them. But, at the same time, I really don't want to take any cash out of the agency for this. We run too tight as it is."

Jennie and Paul both knew as well as I did what the financial situation at the agency was. We ran the business pretty close to the vest, and like most of the smaller agencies, if things suddenly went wrong, like losing Branson, we could be in real trouble. Jennie, as usual, came up with what seemed to be to be the logical solution.

"Look," she said, "why don't we go ahead with the lab testing, including the second one. I think you're right. We've got to validate the ingredients in Cavernite no matter what we do, and from what you've said, this guy at the FDA seems to be hell-bent on two tests, so we may not have a choice."

"I'm afraid so," I said.

"If the product testing turns out all right, then we can do some patient testing, depending on what it costs, and what we can afford. If the patient testing turns out O.K., then I would think our strategy might be to hold a major press conference to announce Cavernite to the world. It's bound to get a lot of publicity, and that should attract some of the drug companies. Brian, after what happened to me in Kentucky I really do believe in this stuff."

I nodded. "Yeah, I guess what we're risking is about a hundred thou or so, and if Cavernite is what we believe it is, we could be looking at millions of dollars. Under the circumstances, I like the odds, except that I'm not sure how we stand with this guy Decker at the FDA. I think I really pissed him off. But, if we hit with some company on this, maybe we can get our up front money back as part of the deal, and they can worry about the testing, the FDA and the marketing. I'll check on getting a second mortgage on the house. I guess you've got to roll the dice sometime."

Paul looked at me. "Brian, I've got some money tucked away. I'd be glad to help out."

"I've got some too," Jennie said.

I shook my head. "Thank you both. I appreciate that, I really do, but I don't want anybody else to take this kind of risk." I was really touched by their offer.

We had gone ahead with a second test on Cavernite. This lab had quoted us twenty to thirty thousand dollars, and I told them we had gotten one test for twenty-two, and would they please keep it in that range. They said they would, and came in at twenty three.

We took those test results, which were basically the same as the report we got from Encino Labs, down to the FDA. Actually J. P. took them down, our rationale being that the less Decker saw of me the better it would be. According to what J. P. said, Decker didn't really give us any points for getting the second test done anyway, since he maintained that we should have done it in the first place, and J. P. couldn't shake him loose on the three to four month schedule. Decker said that since it involved other departments it was pretty much out of his hands. I really think I was being made to pay for the little scene we had in his office. I wondered if I was being totally childish, just because I had this urge to find out where Decker parked his car at the office, and let the air out of his tires. Nah!

Gino Moretti brought the envelope he had gotten from the woman at the FDA back to Koldex and delivered it to Gunderson, who told him to sit down.

Gunderson open it up and quickly read the two reports. The reports gave him the information he needed on Brian McCarthy. He thought for a moment and then turned to Moretti.

"Gino, I have an assignment for you. This is very important, so pay attention."

"Sure, Boss."

"There is a man here in Los Angeles named Brian McCarthy, who runs a small advertising agency. He has apparently discovered something, a medical product that could have a major impact on our business. I will give you his home and office addresses and I want him followed night and day. I need to know where this substance comes from. Do you understand?"

"Yeah, Boss."

"If this requires some additional people, hire them. This is very important. Don't fail on this."

I finally had to take out a second mortgage on the house for fifty grand to pay some of the Cavernite expenses, and to build up a kitty for the patient tests. J. P. and I started interviewing clinics, after I wrote him a check for another thousand dollars for an additional ten hours of his services. Actually, I was not unhappy with J. P. He was doing what I had hired him to do, which was to help me out in a business that I knew very little about. I wondered sometimes if he was orchestrating a little balancing act between Decker and myself, but in a sense that was what he was being paid to do too.

Skip Wilson was the field man in L. A. for a Congressman whose campaign I had worked on. I called him and set up a lunch for the following day. Over a couple of hamburgers I explained the whole situation to him, and asked him what we ought to do about the FDA.

"Well, frankly, Brian, we don't want to ruffle their feathers too much. They can put a lot of road- blocks in the way if they want to. We'll just make a friendly inquiry, and let them know we're interested. Later, if you think you're getting a bad deal, give me a call. But I'd keep a detailed log of conversations or meetings that you have."

I decided to approach two of the drug companies, Koldex and Belmont, and thought I'd see if Monroe had any words of wisdom for me. Besides, I figured I still had some of my ten hours left with him, and I wouldn't be spending any more time with the FDA, at least not at this point.

I needed to make a quick trip down to Kentucky to pick up the samples I needed for testing. I got to the airport the next morning about nine o'clock. There was a man a couple of people behind me in the line at the ticket counter. I don't know why I noticed him except that he was mean looking with this thick head of curly black hair.

When I boarded the plane I saw him again coming down the aisle. Once we arrived in Louisville, he exited the plane right behind me, and I saw him again at the Hertz rental car counter. This was getting a little weird.

I called Jim Adair, told him I was in town and we agreed to meet at the farm the next morning.

I stopped at the restaurant in Cave Junction to get some dinner, and the man with the curly hair entered the restaurant just after I did. This was really getting strange, and I began to get the feeling that I was being followed.

I met Jim the next morning, and we went down in the cave to get the samples I needed. I was back on the plane to Los Angeles that afternoon, and forgot all about the incident.

Chapter Fourteen

I was back in the office the next morning when my phone rang. It was our receptionist.

"I have a Mr. Gunderson calling for you. He says he is with Koldex Corporation."

I picked up the phone. "Hello."

"Mr. McCarthy, my name is Hugo Gunderson. I am President of Koldex Corporation."

"Yes, Mr. Gunderson. What can I do for you?"

"Our company is a major manufacturer of cold remedies."

"Yes, I've heard of you, but we are an ad agency here."

"Yes, I know." The voice was deep with a definite raspy quality to it."

He continued. "There is a rumor going around our industry that you have access to a new product that might be of interest to us."

"Really? Where did you hear that?"

"You know how rumors are, Mr. McCarthy."

"Yes I do, and in this case there might be some truth to it."

"I would like to discuss it with you. When can we talk?

"I don't know, Mr. Gunderson. You are on our list of companies to talk to eventually, but at this point it might be a bit premature."

"Why don't you let me be the judge of that. I will see you at nine o'clock Tuesday morning at my office."

"Do you have any information you can send us ahead of time?"

"We have some lab reports we could send you."

"Send them."

By now I was now really curious about all of this so I agreed. "All right."

"I will fax you directions." The phone went dead.

I decided to take Jennie and Paul along, and we met for an early breakfast at seven o'clock on Tuesday. According to the directions I had received, the Koldex headquarters building was a good hour from our office.

It was definitely out of town. In fact there was not another building near it. Hugo Gunderson obviously liked privacy, because he had built his headquarters literally out in the country. It began to loom up in front of us, a very modern four-story building, built with what appeared to be a dark grey granite material and black glass. As we got closer we could see a much larger one-story building in back of it, which was probably the area where they had their manufacturing and warehousing.

It was obviously designed to be a very high security facility, with a double row of wire fences surrounding the grounds, plainly marked with warning signs in several locations, proclaiming the fact that this was private property, trespassing was not allowed, and that the inner fence was charged with high voltage and was therefore dangerous. The whole effect of the building and the grounds was grim and forbidding-looking.

"It looks more like a prison than a business building," Jennie said "I'm surprised they don't have searchlights and guard towers."

"Yeah," I said. "I wonder why they need all this security for a company that makes and sells cold remedies?"

"From what little I've read about him," Paul said, "this whole complex seems to match Hugo Gunderson's personality. I guess he has a real hang-up about security and privacy."

We drove up to a gate, where a guard checked our names against a list, after which we were given clip-on badges, and directed to the visitor's parking lot, adjacent to the main entrance. My observation of the guards we had seen was that they looked and acted like they had graduated with honors from the Gestapo School of Guard Training. They were not your average, casual industrial guards. I also noticed a guard truck, patrolling the perimeter of the inside fence.

Just in front of the main entrance was a large bronze statue, maybe twenty feet high, identified by a plaque at the base as being Gunther Gunderson, founder. He was a rather formidable looking old gentleman, and fit in pretty well with all the other decor we had seen so far at Koldex headquarters.

The lobby was huge, completely glassed in, and open all the way up to the ceiling, four floors above. It was austerely furnished, the only items of furniture being a few chairs and a couple of sofas over to one side, not far from a receptionist's desk. The rest of the huge room was bare. No product display, nothing. We identified ourselves to the receptionist, and she asked us to be seated. There was also a guard in the area, sitting near the receptionist.

As we walked over to the chairs, I said to Paul and Jennie, "When it comes to security, this place is right up there with Fort Knox." We sat down, and contemplated the view of the backside of Gunther Gunderson's statue.

In about five minutes a middle-aged woman approached us. "I'm Martha Pedersen, Mr. Gunderson's secretary. He is in the middle of a meeting, so it will be a few minutes. I'll be out to get you as soon as possible." No smile. She turned around and marched through a doorway in back of the receptionist's desk. Meanwhile Gunderson was talking to Gino Moretti.

"Gino, we have a situation at the moment. There is a man out in the lobby named Brian McCarthy, who claims to have some sort of miracle overnight cure for colds. I told you about him the other day. I want you to take a look at him, but don't let him see you. I'll have some additional instructions for you after while."

Martha Pederson reappeared in the lobby and led us back to Gunderson's office.

We walked into one of the most amazing offices I have ever seen. The dimensions were big, I would guess maybe seventy by fifty feet.

You could fit my office in there three or four times, and the ceiling went up two stories, adding to the feeling of space.

I heard Jennie murmur, "Wow!"

Martha Pedersen said "Please be seated. Mr. Gunderson will be with you in a moment."

The room was laid out into two areas. The area we were standing in had a setting of eight chairs, spaced around a rectangular conference table. All of the furniture was ebony in color. Several feet from where we were standing, there was a second floor level, about a foot or so higher, almost like a low stage. Sitting on that level was the biggest desk I've ever seen, also ebony. Everything in the room was dark or black, and the illumination in the room came from a series of pinpoint beams, located high above in the ceiling. The windows were tinted, and I guessed that they were one- way glass.

Hugo Gunderson was sitting behind the massive desk, absorbed in some papers in front of him, or pretending to be. After a moment or two, he looked over our way, and then got up and walked toward us. The pictures we had seen of him didn't do him justice. He wasn't just big, he was massive, massive like the lobby and the office and the desk. His head was totally bald, or shaved that way, and it gleamed in the light coming down from the ceiling above. He was dressed in a black suit, with a gray shirt and a bright red tie.

It was pretty obvious that everything we had been exposed to so far had been carefully orchestrated to create an atmosphere of intimidation for any visitors that Gunderson might have. And it did.

He stopped at the edge of the step-down and looked down at us. "Mr. McCarthy?" The voice was deep, hoarse and emotionless, as it had been over the phone. He looked directly at me as he spoke, so somehow he already knew who I was.

"Brian McCarthy," I said, standing my ground. We both stood still for a moment. Finally he stepped down to our level, and walked over to where we were waiting. I nodded at Jennie and Paul. "And these are my associates, Jennie McCarthy, and Paul Miller."

"How do you do," he rumbled, shaking hands with each of us. I judged him to be about six feet, six inches tall, and big; big shoulders, big frame, large head. He weighed at least two hundred and fifty pounds, but I had also noticed that he was quite graceful when he had stepped down to our level. He wasn't fat, just big, and he carried all of that weight quite well. "Please sit down," he commanded, gesturing at the conference table.

We all took chairs, and sat down. Gunderson and I stared at each other briefly. He was wearing a pair of dark sunglasses, which I didn't care for. I like to look at people's eyes when I'm talking to them. Eyes can tell you a lot about a person. I decided to break the ice.

"Did you receive the package of reports that I sent you, Mr. Gunderson?"

"Yes, I did, Mr. McCarthy." Silence again. This was real gamesmanship. Gunderson finally broke the silence.

"I would like to buy your little company."

"The ad agency?"

Gunderson snorted. "No, of course back. I have no interest in that. I'm talking about McCarthy Drugs, or whatever you call it."

"I'm not sure that's for sale."

"Everything is for sale for a price."

"Yes, I suppose so. How much are you willing to offer us for it?"

"I really don't know yet. I need some more information first, and I would like to see this cave."

"How do you know a cave is involved?"

"I know that and I know where it is located. In Kentucky."

This surprised me.

"How did you find this out?"

"Things like that are not difficult to find out, Mr. McCarthy. When can we see the cave?"

I thought this over for a moment. Obviously anyone who was serious about making a deal would want to go through the cave.

"We can make arrangements for some time next week. Have you ever been down in a cave, Mr. Gunderson?"

"Once, when I was a small child."

"I see. Well, some of the passageways are very small. It would be impossible for you to get through them."

"Then I'll bring someone along to go into the cave."

"Who would that be?"

"I don't know, but I will bring someone."

We agreed on a date the following week and Jennie and I left the building.

"What do you think?" I asked.

Jennie shook her head. "That man is something else, Brian. Frankly he scares me."

"I suspect his bark is worse than his bite."

"I don't know. I hope you're right."

A couple of days ago Jan Thompson had brought in some background material on Koldex and Belmont, and I had routed copies of the data to Jennie and Paul. The two companies were an interesting contrast, in almost every way.

Koldex was a public company, traded on the over the counter market, and headquartered a little North of Los Angeles. It had really started out as a single drug store out in the valley, owned by Gunther Gunderson, which he built into a local chain of drug stores, and finally into a company specializing in cold remedies. Hugo Gunderson, son of the founder, had taken over the business upon the death of his father a few years ago, and had expanded the business dramatically. He had moved the company out of the retail business, selling the stores, and had concentrated on the cold remedy market, building the stature of the company until Koldex had become a household name in the national market.

Actually the details on the company and Hugo Gunderson were pretty sketchy. Gunderson came across as a mysterious character, very private, someone who avoided publicity, and you got the idea that some of the things he had done over the years were a little suspect. A couple of the magazine articles used words like "brutal" and "ruthless". The comments by his competitors were guarded, but left you with the feeling that he was perhaps feared, but certainly not admired.

There were a couple of pictures of Gunderson in the biographical stuff, although they appeared to be candid shots rather than posed, and from the photos he appeared to be a very large man, completely bald, grim and unsmiling. The one thing that seemed a little surprising was that Gunderson had apparently not chosen to expand the company's range of products beyond cold remedies. It was like he wanted to dominate that market to the exclusion of anything else, and Koldex did have the largest market share, slightly larger than Belmont's.

Belmont Pharmaceutical, Los Angeles based, on the other hand seemed to be a direct contrast. It was the All-American company and James Harrison, its president, was the All-American boy. The company was also publicly traded on the New York Stock Exchange, was considerably larger than Koldex, and had a much broader base in its product line than just cold remedies.

James Harrison was a guy who had risen from the ranks. He had joined the company out of a small college in the middle-west, starting in the sales force, and had worked his way up to the top. The pictures of him portrayed a very pleasant looking, capable, middle-aged executive.

Jennie and I had finalized our wedding plans for the twentieth of November. We decided that by having it in late November we could have a combination vacation, ski trip to Mammoth, and honeymoon. The ceremony would be very simple, held at home, with a few friends and co-workers invited. We didn't want to make it a big occasion, especially since it was the second time around for both of us.

I finally had to take out a second mortgage on the house for fifty grand to pay some of the Cavernite expenses, and to build up a kitty for the patient tests. J. P. and I started interviewing clinics. Fortunately for our project it was now Fall, and we were going into the cold season, so the clinics didn't see any major problem in finding suitable subjects for the test. There would be plenty of runny noses around.

Jennie, of course, was our unofficial prophet, and wanted to give Cavernite to friends and/or employees who caught cold, or for that matter to anybody she saw using a Kleenex, but I kept telling her that it was too risky. If they came down with anything from a fever sore to the bubonic plague, they'd probably go get a lawyer and sue us.

The quotes we got from the clinics varied somewhat, but we finally settled for fifteen hundred dollars per patient at the Jerald Clinic in Thousand Oaks, and they agreed to keep us immediately up to date on the results as they happened. They also wanted to be paid up front, but settled for a partial payment.

We had gotten the FDA tentatively to at least consider follow-up exams at three and eight months, and I sure as hell wasn't going to pay in advance for a service that wouldn't be performed until eight months from now. We also made it clear that the patient tests wouldn't be funded nor would they start until we had heard back from the FDA on the lab test reports.

I got a phone call from J. P. on a Tuesday morning.

"Good morning, Brian," he said. "I just received a phone call from Decker down at the *administration*. He would like to schedule a meeting with us at his office on Thursday morning at ten o'clock. Is that acceptable to you?"

I glanced at my calendar, saw that there was already an appointment at that time, but quickly decided I could get it re-scheduled for this. "You bet," I said. "Did he give you any idea as to what the result was?"

"No, he gave me no indication whatsoever over the phone. He said that would prefer to discuss the matter in person. That's not unusual with Decker, by the way."

"Hm. Well, I guess I'll see you down there on Thursday." I suspected that J. P. knew more than he was telling me, and I figured that might be good news. My logic was that if the news was bad, then J. P. might have gotten some inkling of it, and would have tried to prepare me for it. Just looking at the background of the two companies, it struck me that dealing with Belmont might be a more agreeable experience. On the other hand, it was obvious that Cavernite would have more of an impact on Koldex, since their business was almost entirely cold remedies, and it would seem certain to have an effect on their sales.

Jennie and I were at the Koldex building at nine for a Wednesday morning appointment we had with Gunderson. and were shown promptly into his office.

Without any preamble he started in on us.

"Mr. McCarthy, I have been very patient with you, but quite frankly I am running out of patience."

"I appreciate that Mr. Gunderson, but there is a lot to do, and it all takes time."

"Like what," he demanded.

"Well, like product testing to determine just exactly what substances the medicine contains. The FDA wanted two separate tests conducted. Then after the tests are examined and approved by the FDA we have to start patient testing. Unfortunately, all of this takes time. You have had to deal with the FDA and should know what's involved."

"On the other hand, if you signed an agreement with us, we would have handled all of those details, and probably a lot faster. One of the problems is that you are an unknown quantity to the FDA, and that slows up everything."

"There is probably some truth in that, I suppose," I replied.

He pulled a folder out of is desk and handed it to me.

"All you have to do is sign these and we will take care of all your problems, Mr. McCarthy."

"Well, I'll think it over, but I can't sign them without having my attorney take a look at them."

"All right. Do that. And let's plan on having them back here, signed, in three days."

"We'll see." I replied.

"Mr. McCarthy, I told you I am losing patience with you, and you really don't want that to happen."

"In that case, what happens?"

"I don't think you really want to know, Mr. McCarthy, but unpleasant things, very unpleasant things could happen to you, or," he pointed at Jennie, "to members of your family."

I jumped to my feet. "What happens between you and me is between us, but don't ever threaten my fiancee again. Ever! This meeting is over."

"You've been warned. Mr. McCarthy. I'll have you escorted to your car."

He hit a buzzer on his desk and the door behind opened and a man walked in.

Brian's eyes widened. It was the man with the dark curly hair.

"This is Gino Moretti, my assistant." Gunderson said.

Brian pointed at the man. "That's the guy who followed me down to Louisville." he exclaimed.

Gunderson laughed. "How do you think I found out where the cave was?"

"That sounds like something you might do. I don't think we have any further business to discuss. Let's get out of here Jennie." Brian started for the door, but Moretti stepped in from of him.

"I'll escort you out."

"I don't need you to tell me where my car is parked."

Moretti grabbed Brian's arm. "Oh yes you do."

At this point Brian was furious. He landed a hard punch in Moretti's stomach, doubling him over. "Get out of my way."

Moetti snarled at him thru clenched teeth, "You'll pay for that."

Brian ignored him, grabbed Jennie's hand and they walked quickly back to the lobby and out the front door.

"Sorry to put you through that, babe."

"It's OK Brian. Calm down."

J. P. and I assembled in Decker's office on Thursday, and went through the preliminary greetings. Decker had a copy of each of the reports I had given him from the labs on the desk in front of him, and looked rather grim.

"Well, Mr. McCarthy," he said, "our departments have reviewed the test results and have come to a conclusion."

Don't fidget, McCarthy, I told myself. "We're very anxious to hear what the results are, Mr. Decker."

He nodded. "First of all, we are dealing with very unusual circumstances, Mr. McCarthy. When a drug or a medicine is developed from scratch, which is the usual situation, we, and the pharmaceutical company, know exactly what the ingredients and contents are, where they came from, and just what percent of each element is contained in the medication. In a case like this, however, there are a lot of unknowns, including this one element that had to be identified. We also don't know how this medication - I believe you call it Cavernite? - will hold up under the conditions that exist in retail pharmacies. A lot of unknowns."

I glanced over at J. P., who seemed to be taking all of this calmly, and I took my clue from him. I just nodded, figuring that whatever I said would probably be the wrong thing anyway.

Decker continued. "Our conclusion from the test reports is that there would appear to be no harmful substance in this vegetation, if administered in moderate dosage. However, we should like the patient tests done in groups of two or three rather than all at once or in large groups. That will allow us to take swift action in suspending the testing in case there should be a problem of some kind. Also I expect Mr. Monroe to assist in that monitoring process. In any event we cannot begin patient testing until we know just what this unknown substance is."

"Then," he said, "if this medication performs as you say it does, under these clinical controls and with supervision, and has no side effects, we will grant you permission to continue patient testing. But we want to make it clear that the early results must be very carefully monitored, and we want you to keep us constantly and immediately informed of all developments."

The news was good, which was no doubt why Decker looked so unhappy, either that or his family had just been kidnapped by cannibals.

I breathed a sigh of relief. "That's really good news, Mr. Decker. We have interviewed several clinics, and have tentatively picked the Jerald Clinic in Thousand Oaks. Also we are ready to further test Cavernite to determine just what this unknown element is, and will conclude that before we start patient testing. Does that sound all right?"

He tilted his head and peered at over his glasses for a few seconds. "Yes, I believe that will be acceptable. However, I want J. P. to monitor each patient and keep me informed, particularly if any kind of a problem arises." That probably meant more checks for good old J. P. These guys sure were in tight. I was beginning to think that if J.P. and I were stranded on a tropical island that J. P. would end up with all of the coconuts.

"That's fine, Mr. Decker." I managed to force a thin, sickly smile. "We'll stay in close touch."

J. P. was smiling as we left the office. "Well, Brian, that's a big hurdle we just got over."

"Yeah, I guess it was, but Decker looked like he just lost his best friend. I think he gets his kicks out of turning products down. The watch dog of the nation."

"He's a very cautious person, Brian, and I think he is still unconvinced of the merits of the product. Hopefully the patient testing will change his attitude."

We decided to drive out to the Jerald Clinic right away, where we had a meeting with Dr. Holmes, the director, and concluded the final arrangements for the first twenty-five patients.

The procedure was fairly complex. The patient would be admitted on day one, would fill out all the necessary forms on their medical history, and would be given a complete physical. On day two they would be given one dose of Cavernite in the morning, consisting of a stem and the bud, and then would be given a second identical dose that evening. On day two the patient would be given a second physical, and released if everything was O.K. A telephone follow-up would be made once a week after that for four weeks, and then another physical would be conducted at the clinic in three months. I told Dr. Holmes that we could not start with the patients until we completed the additional testing on Cavernite.

I called Jim Adair to tell him to bring out some more samples.

"How many you reckon you'll need, Brian?"

"Why don't you cut off about eighty-five stalks, Jim." We had decided to give the clinic enough Cavernite to test all of the patients and use the other ten stalks for the other test. That would also give us an opportunity to see if there was any deterioration in either its appearance or its effectiveness over the length of the tests, which looked like would take about two to four weeks. That was J. P.'s idea, which seemed like a good one.

"I'll get over there tomorrow," Jim said. "By the way, Will 'n I been pokin' around down in the cave some, Brian."

"Really? What did you find?" I felt a pang of jealousy. I would have loved to have been there with them.

"Not much, Brian. We took some ropes and a rubber raft, and went down where that fall off place was. You remember that?"

"Yeah, I sure do."

"Well, we did find one other tunnel down there, but it petered out pretty quick. I'm afraid there just ain't much else down there in that cave, Brian. Don't seem to be any other way to get in or out either, 'cept mebbe for some little holes we didn't see where them pack rats might get in."

"Well, I'm sort of disappointed, Jim, but I appreciate your checking it out. Send me a bill for your time."

"I'll do that, Brian."

We had the fresh samples the following Tuesday, and immediately delivered them to the clinic, keeping them under constant temperature control.

The first three patients checked in on Wednesday, went through their physicals, and were given the Cavernite on Thursday. I couldn't stand the suspense, and was at the clinic at eight o'clock sharp on Friday morning. When I walked in the lobby, J. P. was sitting there waiting. I had to give him credit for being on the job.

"Any news?" I asked.

He shook his head. "I'm waiting for the Director. I believe he has just arrived, and is probably checking on the patients at this moment.

Christ was I nervous! This must be like having a baby.

The phone finally buzzed, the receptionist picked it up and nodded. "Dr. Holmes can see you now," she said.

We walked down the hall to his office, knocked and opened the door. He was sitting behind his desk, with what were obviously medical reports of some sort spread out in front of him.

"Come in gentlemen. I have some news for you."

Not good news, not bad news, just news. Why did people love to string things out. It was like pulling the wings off a fly.

He continued. "I must say that when you gentlemen first approached us on this project I was quite skeptical. It just didn't seem to make any sense, despite the lab reports and your own personal experience. But there is only one way to find out, and that is through scientific investigation."

I forced a smile. "Doctor Holmes, frankly I'm sitting here dying to know just what the hell happened. Can we get to the bottom line?"

He smiled back. "Of course, Mr. McCarthy. So far the results are excellent. All three patients seem to be completely cured of their colds, and appear to have no side effects. In fact, they are delighted with the results. Of course, we haven't given them their post medication physical yet, so we really need to see how that comes out. But so far I must say I am impressed."

J. P. and I shook hands. I felt like I had just won the lottery, which I probably had. "That's great news, Doctor. I would appreciate it if someone could call me at the office as soon as possible with the results of the physicals."

"Yes," J. P. added. "Call both of us. I will need to relay the information to the FDA immediately."

"Certainly," the Doctor said. "Also we hope to have three more patients in on Monday, and additional patients should be coming in regularly after that. I would imagine all twenty five should be through here and completed in the next two or three weeks."

"Terrific," I said. "We'll stay in close touch, Doctor. And J. P., you'll be calling Decker?"

"The minute I have the information," he replied. "He's usually in his office by about nine, but it would be better if I contacted him after the physicals are completed. He'll want to have the complete data anyway."

"We should have the results on the physicals by ten or ten thirty," Holmes said. "I'll call both of you just as soon as we know."

I was already beginning to make mental plans for the press conference. When I got out to the lobby I called the office and asked for Jennie.

"Jennie, it looks like we just hit the jackpot, babe!"

"Really, Brian?"

"Yeah. The first three patients tests went perfectly. They're all cured and feeling great. We won't have the results on this morning's physical exams until about ten or ten-thirty, but I really don't think there will be any problems."

I could tell she was as excited as I was. "That's fantastic, Brian."

"Yeah. We've got to get together and start talking about a press conference. Get a hold of Paul, and see if he can come in today.

"Right. I'll call him as soon as I'm off the phone."

"You're off now, and I'm on my way in to the office. Love ya!" I hung up the phone and went out to my car. It was time to get things moving.

Later on that same morning Dr. Holmes called, and reported that all three patients had received their post medication physicals. All of them seemed to be in excellent condition, and were quite enthusiastic about the medication.

Then, on Tuesday night of the following week, Jennie and I had just walked into the house after dinner when the phone rang. It was about eight-thirty.

I picked it up. "Hello?"

"Brian? This is J. P. I just received a call from the clinic. They started three more patients on the testing today, and two of them are apparently quite ill, and were vomiting."

"What? My God! What's the problem, J. P.?" I felt like someone had just punched me in the stomach. Jennie came back in the room with a questioning look on her face, probably because of my tone of voice.

"I don't really have any further details as yet, Brian. I just received the call from the Jerald clinic, and I wanted to let you know first. I'm on my way over to the clinic right now."

"I'll meet you there." I hung up the phone.

"What's the matter, Brian?" Jennie asked.

"That was J. P. They started three more patients on the testing today at the clinic, and two of them got sick. I'm going to meet J. P. there."

"I'm going with you."

The clinic was about thirty minutes away, and all we could do on the way over was speculate on what had happened, but I had this bad feeling.

"Damn it, Jennie, I knew things were going too good. I kept thinking something like this would happen. If we've gotten a reaction of some kind to the medicine, not only can we kiss the money goodbye we've put into this, but probably the whole project as well. And you know, the sad part is that I really thought this stuff would be a great thing for people who get colds."

"Brian, let's don't jump to any conclusions, O.K.? We really don't know what happened yet. It may not have anything to do with Cavernite."

"Well, hopefully we'll know something pretty soon."

We pulled up in front of the clinic and ran into the reception area. I explained to the receptionist who I was and why I was there, and ask her who was in charge at night. She said it was Dr. Sawyer, and rang his extension.

A few seconds later a young man in one of those white medical frocks showed up in the lobby.

"I'm Dr. Sawyer."

"I'm Brian McCarthy, Doctor, and this is Jennie Carson. I understand we have some kind of a problem with two of the patients we're testing."

"Why don't we go back to my office," the doctor said.

"O.K." I turned to the receptionist. "A Mr. Monroe is on his way over here. Would you send him back when he arrives?"

We went into a small cubby-hole of an office down the hall, with barely room for two folding chairs for Jennie and me.

"Tell me what happened," I said.

"Well, two of the patients we are testing for you became quite ill this evening, about seven o'clock, I believe it was."

"Have you looked at them?"

"Yes, they were vomiting, and running a slight fever, but they seem to be a little better now. However, I called Mr. Monroe right away to let him know about the situation."

"Do you have any idea what caused this?"

"Not yet, but we're trying to determine the cause."

"Did all three of the patients receive both doses of Cavernite today?" I asked.

"Yes, they did."

Jennie spoke up. "Could it have been caused by something else, like something they ate?"

"I would hardly think so, although we haven't checked on that as yet."

J. P. walked in at that point, and I quickly filled him in on the conversation so far.

"Have you been in contact with Dr. Holmes?" J. P. asked the doctor.

"I tried, but he wasn't at home."

"Doesn't he have a pager?" J. P. asked.

"Yes. I haven't tried that."

"Don't you think you should?" I asked. "This is a pretty serious matter. Certainly to us if not to you." This young doctor seemed to be pretty nonchalant about everything, and my Irish temper was starting to flare up.

Before he could answer, Jennie spoke up again. "Do you have some record of what the patients had for dinner?"

"The dietician does," Sawyer responded.

"Doesn't it seem like that would be worth checking out?" she asked. Sawyer was getting nervous now, and it was obvious that he had not been on top of the situation. He picked up the phone and dialed a number. "Miriam, this is Dr. Sawyer. As you know, we are presently testing three patients for McCarthy Pharmaceutical. Two of them became ill this evening. Could you bring down the records on their meals for today? Thank you."

A couple of minutes later a woman walked in his office with some papers in her hand.

"Miriam, these people are from McCarthy Pharmaceutical. Let's see what you have."

We all nodded. Miriam was about five eight, and weighed at least two hundred pounds. Thinking back, it seemed to me that the dietitians we had around when I was in high school were all on the heavy side. Made you wonder how much they really knew about meal planning.

We waited while Dr. Sawyer looked over the papers. Finally he nodded. "This is interesting. It seems that two of the patients had salmon for dinner, and the other one had beef."

"The two that got sick both had salmon?" Jennie asked.

"That's right," the doctor said.

"Then that's probably it!" I said.

"We should certainly consider that as a possibility." Dr. Sawyer said. He was sure being casual with our future.

"Did anyone else in the clinic beside the two patients have salmon for dinner?" Jennie asked.

"I really don't know," he said.

"Who would know?" I asked.

"The chef would know," Dr. Sawyer said.

It was pretty obvious to me that all of these questions should have been dealt with long before we arrived at the clinic.

Miriam looked at him, rather sheepishly, I thought. "The chef wasn't feeling well, doctor. He went home early."

"Well, damn it, call him, and find out what he had for dinner." Jennie said.

We waited while Dr. Sawyer looked up the number and dialed it. "Ramon, I understand you're not feeling well." Pause. "That's too bad. Did you eat dinner here at the clinic?" Pause "What did you eat?" Pause. "Salmon" Pause "Well, two of our patients came down sick this evening, and it seems that they had the salmon for dinner also. Is there some of the fish still around the kitchen? All right. Well, take care of yourself, Ramon."

He looked at us. "Well, as you heard, our chef had salmon for dinner, and seems to have the same symptoms as the patients. Some of the salmon is still in the kitchen, so we can have it tested."

"When?" I asked.

"We'll contact a lab tomorrow."

J. P. shook his head. "We had best get to the bottom of this as quickly as possible. I would strongly suggest that the salmon be tested tonight."

"Absolutely!" I said.

Dr. Sawyer finally agreed that he would find a way to get that done right away.

The three of us left the Doctor's tiny office, and huddled in the lobby. We were all feeling better about the situation, but not about the way it had been handled, and concluded that J. P. should have that conversation with Dr. Holmes in the morning. They should have investigated the menu immediately, and Dr. Holmes should have been reached as soon as the problem first arose.

J. P. called the next morning. "Brian, Dr. Holmes and I have had a lengthy discussion about the way that situation was addressed yesterday. He's as unhappy with the way it was handled as we are, and assured me that they would maintain tighter controls for the remainder of the testing."

"Yeah, well Holmes ought to be unhappy," I replied. "I sure as hell am. That was really bush league."

"He is concerned, I assure you, Brian. Also, you know I'm going to have to report this incident to Decker," J. P. said.

"I know. I guess you have to. That ought to make his day,"

"Well, it shouldn't really affect anything in the long run. We'll just continue on with the testing. The illness wasn't anything that our medicine caused. It also turned out that another employee at the clinic had eaten the salmon, and she came down with the same symptoms, so I believe that pretty well verifies the situation. After all, four individuals became ill, only two of whom were taking the medication, the other two being clinic employees. The only factor they had in common was that they all had consumed the salmon."

"You're right, but I don't know if Decker will look at it that way. Let me know what he says. So you feel that everything is under control at Jerald now, J. P.?" I asked.

"Yes, I sincerely do, Brian. Jerald is a very reputable clinic, and Dr. Holmes and I are both very embarrassed by this whole incident. I assure you that all matters will be handled quite professionally in the future."

Chapter Fifteen

J ennie and I got married, as planned, on the fourth of November, one of the great days in my life. It was very simple, a civil ceremony at our house, with about fifteen or so people, close friends and a few people from the office.

That evening, after everyone had left, I picked Jennie up and carried her over the threshold, into the bedroom that is, and we were about to make love for the first time as Mr. and Mrs. Brian McCarthy.

"Jennie McCarthy. What a fine soundin' name that is. It fairly rolls off the tongue," I said, in a terrible imitation of an Irish brogue.

Her accent was probably worse than mine. "Aye lad. A fine, bonnie name it is."

"I really love you, Jennie. But I have to tell you, bonnie is a Scotch word, not Irish."

"I love you, Brian, and who cares." She stopped for a moment. "Brian, I want to ask you something."

"Anything, my love. What is it?"

"How would you feel about having a baby?"

I thought for a moment. "Jennie, I don't think its biologically possible for me to have a baby, but I'm certainly willing to try."

She smiled, indulging my pathetic attempt at humor. "I'm serious, Brian. We've never talked about it, and I wouldn't want to unless it was something you wanted too."

"Do you want to have a baby, Jennie?"

She just nodded.

"Do you really want to have a baby?"

Her eyes were big and round, and she looked so serious. "Yes, Brian, I really do want to have a baby."

I reached over and pulled her closer to me, curling one hand around one of her lovely breasts. "Well then, I think we're just going to have to try harder." And we did try. Right then.

You know, when you're newlyweds, like Jennie and I were, and you're sexually active, like Jennie and I were, you sometimes wonder later which time was it that got Jennie pregnant. Not that it really matters, just idle curiosity I guess.

In the meantime we had the secondary tests done on Cavernite to determine what the unknown substance in it was. It turned out not only to be harmless, but was actually beneficial to the process of attacking a cold.

I had J. P. take the report down to my dear friend at the FDA. According to J. P., Decker was somewhat relieved to get the information, and we had now crossed another hurdle and were cleared to begin patient testing, which we had done. Everything went along great, and we were now ready for the "big" press conference.

Jennie, Bob Wagner and I headed for New York in January for the press conference. J. P. had pushed hard to come along, but I just didn't want to spend the money on either his time or expenses, so I turned him down.

We had set it up in a medium sized conference room in one of the mid-town New York hotels, and ended up with twenty-two people, including one from the Journal, two from wire services, and one each from the New York Times, Business Week and Newsweek, which really wasn't bad. I think Bob had to pull a lot of strings even to get that kind of turn out. The other sixteen reporters were from an assortment of trade magazines.

Of course it was the consumer press that we were really after. They reach a much larger audience and can react a lot faster. If the reporter and the editor think it's a hot story, you could see an article as quickly as the following day in the Journal or the Times, whereas the trade magazines, mostly monthlies, can take weeks before anything finally appears in print.

We played the whole thing as straight as possible, and started out by telling them simply that, through an unusual set of circumstances, a substance had been discovered that appeared to offer an overnight cure for the common cold. We gave them a brief description of the substance, and described in general terms where Cavernite had been discovered. Following that, we had representatives from the two labs that had tested Cavernite give their credentials and present their findings.

Then Dr. Holmes got up and described the results of the tests on the twenty-five patients, including the ninety-day follow-up physicals. No one had experienced any kind of problem, and in fact, no one had even experienced any cold symptoms since then, although we really didn't know whether that was coincidence or not.

Once the reporters began to get the picture, the level of interest started picking up. Right away, the consumer press zeroed in on where Cavernite came from. I handled that part of the presentation, and as politely as I could, pretty much stonewalled them, telling them simply that the substance grew in a cavern somewhere in the midwestern part of the United States. They kept digging at me, but I just continued diverting the questions back to the medicinal value of our discovery, adding that for security reasons we were not prepared to divulge the location.

We were very careful in the way we handled the FDA, making it as clear as possible that we had been working closely with them, but also making it just as clear that we did not yet have a clearance from the government on Cavernite, but were still following their procedures meticulously, and were working toward an approval at some future date.

When everyone had finally left, Jennie, Bob and I went downstairs to the hotel restaurant for lunch.

"Well, what do you think?" I asked Bob.

He shrugged. "Sometimes it's hard to say with a press conference, Brian. They seemed to be interested, and we probably would have gotten more reaction if we had felt that we wanted to tell them more about the cave."

"Yeah, but the more I thought about that idea the less I liked it," I said. "We've got a gate and a padlock on the cave, but that wouldn't really keep anyone out who wanted to get in badly enough. We're going to have to give some more thought to security down there, now that it's becoming public knowledge."

"Everything considered, I think we played it right on the cave. As far a reaction, we'll just have to wait and see what happens," Bob continued.

The reaction started slowly, and then began to build. The first article of any substance appeared in Business Week. They speculated a little about the origin of the medicine, and just what and who McCarthy Pharmaceuticals might be, but did a really good job on the patient testing. They concluded the article by questioning what the result of Cavernite might be on existing drug companies, mentioning Koldex in particular. This aspect of their article caught the attention of some other business publications, and additional articles starting appearing.

The phone calls started coming in, a couple at first, and then growing in volume. Jennie and I handled all of the calls personally, and for a few days it took up a lot of our time, until the number of calls started to slow down again. We got calls from newspapers, stock analysts, potential investors, and drug companies, some of which were foreign based. Of course, we also heard from the usual number of kooks.

The kooks were something else. They ranged from a guy who claimed the whole thing was part of a Communist plot to ruin the health care structure in this country, to people with runny noses and sore throats, who demanded immediate treatment.

We handled all the calls from drug companies the same way, replying that we might be interested in discussing Cavernite with them, but at the right level, and to call us back when that could be arranged.

Koldex was one of the early callers, and was obviously interested, because after they got our initial response, I received a call back the same day from Hugo Gunderson. The voice on the phone was strange, sort of hoarse and deep, almost whispery, and devoid of emotion. He almost sounded like one of those electronic recordings you hear nowadays.

"Good day, Mr. McCarthy, we have seen some newspaper reports on the press conference you had. We would be interested in getting some more information on this product, and would like to have some samples as soon as possible."

"Mr. Gunderson, I'm afraid that it won't be possible to send you samples at this early stage in our discussions. However, we would be interested in sitting down and talking about it in more detail."

"How do I know that this product is authentic, Mr. McCarthy?"

"At this point you don't, Mr. Gunderson. I don't know what you have read about it, but I'll bring along copies of lab reports and the patient testing we have done so far, both conducted by totally qualified organizations, which may give you some of the information you are looking for."

"Hm. Why don't you send us copies of those reports by express mail, so that we can look at them ahead of time." The way Gunderson put it it wasn't a request, it was a demand, and obviously he was a guy who was used to getting his way.

I thought about that for a minute. I guess we were going to have to begin to divulge information on Cavernite some time.

"Sure. We can do that. I'll Fed Ex them out to you today, and then we can get together. How would next Tuesday be?"

"Tuesday, nine o'clock. My office." He hung up the phone. I sat there for a minute, slightly in shock and then walked into Jennie's office.

"Well, I just got off the phone with Gunderson from Koldex. What a cold fish! But he seems to be pretty interested, and we have a meeting set up with him for next Tuesday in Los Angeles."

"What did he have to say?" Jennie asked.

"Not much really. He wanted some samples of Cavernite, but I told him it was too early for that. I did agree to Fed Ex him copies of the lab reports. I tell you, Jennie, he sounds like one tough son-of-a-bitch."

"Well, I guess that's his reputation." She waved a slip of paper at me. "Here's some good news. While I was on the phone with someone else we got a message from a Marla O'Conner at Belmont. Apparently she's the assistant to the President, and wants more information on Cavernite."

"Why don't you let me take that one. Since we already have a meeting with Koldex for next Tuesday, I'll see if I can work something out with Belmont for the same day in the afternoon."

"What's the matter, Brian." Jennie asked. "Are you afraid I'll screw it up?"

She was baiting me. "No Jennie, I just thought it would be easier if one of us coordinated the trip, in case there are any scheduling problems."

"Oh. O.K." Then she gave me this big grin.

I called the number Jennie had given me, and a female voice came on the line, very crisp, very efficient. "Marla O'Conner speaking."

"Good morning, Miss O'Conner. This is Brian McCarthy. You had called regarding some information on Cavernite, I believe."

"Yes, Mr. McCarthy. Mr. Harrison saw an article on it, and asked me to get some additional information if we could."

"Certainly, Miss O'Conner. However, let me make a suggestion. We're going to be back at our office in the west coast next week, talking to another Pharmaceutical company, and perhaps could work out a schedule to see Mr. Harrison as well. Quite frankly, Belmont is on a small list of companies we would like to discuss the product with. What would the possibility of a meeting next Tuesday afternoon be?"

"I'd have to check with Mr. Harrison on that. Let me do that and I'll call you back."

About twenty minutes later she was back on the phone. "It looks like Tuesday would be fine. How about two o'clock?"

"That's great. We'll see you then. Thank you."

Right then J. P. called. He had been in touch with Arnold Decker at the FDA, who had seen some of the publicity.

"What was his reaction?" I asked.

"Approximately what I had anticipated," J. P. said. "He would rather we had not had the press conference, but on the other hand, there didn't seem to be anything that he could take great exception to."

"How about the problem with the two patients?"

"Actually he didn't seem to be very concerned."

"Well, that's good news. We're getting a lot of calls here, J. P., and we've got a couple of meetings set up for next week."

"Who are you seeing?"

"Koldex and Belmont."

"Be careful with Koldex, Brian. Maybe I should go with you."

I knew J. P. was dying to get more involved, but I just didn't see any reason for it at this point. "I think we can handle the initial contact, but I'll talk to you when we get back."

"Please do, and good luck."

I walked into Jennie's office. "O.K. We've got Koldex on Tuesday morning and Belmont that afternoon. Can you check your schedule and Paul's?"

"Listen, as long as you're coordinating the trip, why don't you handle that too," Jennie said. She was really in an ornery mood this morning.

"O.K." I replied, and started to leave.

"Just kidding, Brian. I'll do it." Actually we weren't much on formality or titles around the shop. Everybody kind of did what needed to be done, so we all pretty much handled our own correspondence and phone calls and such. Jennie just enjoyed giving me a hard time once in a while. She smiled sweetly and batted her eyes at me. "I suppose now that we're going to be millionaires we can fly first class?"

I laughed. "Until the checks start rolling in, I think we'll stay in the back of the plane with the rest of the poor folks."

"Cheapskate!"

Chapter Sixteen

Paul, Jennie and I arrived back in Los Angeles from the press conference on the 2nd of February, which is Ground Hogs Day, if you're interested, and you are probably not. It was late in the evening by the time we got home.

I was in the office the next morning when my phone rang. It was Gunderson.

"Mr. McCarthy, I have been reading more reports about your press conference, and you have not returned those signed papers to me."

"The purpose of our press conference was to stir up interest in our company, and it has done that."

Silence again. This was real gamesmanship.

"Do you have any questions, Mr. Gunderson?"

"Yes, I do," he replied. "How much do you want for your company, Mr. McCarthy?"

"Which company, Mr. Gunderson?"

"Your pharmaceutical company, Mr. McCarthy. I would hardly be interested in your little advertising agency. We've been through this before."

"Let me tell you what we are doing, Mr. Gunderson. We are in the process of having discussions with a limited number of corporations. If they are truly interested in Cavernite, then what we are asking them to do is to outline the terms of their offer."

"How can you seriously suggest that, Mr. McCarthy? I haven't even seen a sample of this vegetation." His voice took on a harder edge, becoming more sibilant, more emotional.

"That's quite true," I said. "But you have seen the lab reports. I would suggest that you formulate your offer based on the assumption that Cavernite is everything that we say it is. Obviously before you sign any final documents you would have the opportunity to satisfy yourself in every way as to the vegetation itself and the source."

He scowled. "That is preposterous."

"You are taking no risk, Mr. Gunderson. You will have the opportunity to perform all of the due diligence that you desire, and you will be going down to the cave where it grows." I was starting to enjoy this. "However, if you are interested in buying McCarthy Pharmaceutical, or in making some arrangement to obtain Cavernite on an exclusive basis, I would like to have your offer in writing. Let's see. Today is Tuesday. I would like to have it one week from next Tuesday. If we feel that your offer is reasonable, then we can continue further negotiations. We want to separate the buyers from the shoppers."

He snorted. "You can't be serious."

"I realize that the final arrangements will take some time, but we would like to determine who is serious at this point and who is not. I do not have the time, the resources or the inclination to get into pharmaceuticals, but I do have something that should be of great value to someone like yourself who is already in the business."

He seemed to be rather agitated. I don't think he was used to having people dictate terms to him, and he was trying to control himself. His tone was venomous, and he literally hissed the words. "I don't really care for the way you do business, Mr. McCarthy. But I do intend to buy your company, and I want to make that perfectly clear. There are also a couple of other things that you should be aware of. First of all, if you are concerned about the confidentiality of the location of your cave, don't be. I am quite aware that it is located on the old Thomas Farm in Cave Junction, Kentucky."

"Yes, you told me that."

"Your announcement to the press about Cavernite has done a great deal of damage to my company. I presume you are aware that we are a publicly traded company?"

"Yes, I am, Mr. Gunderson."

"Do you know what has happened to our stock since you had your press conference?"

I shook my head. "Frankly I don't. The stock market is not something I have much interest in."

"Well, for your information, prior to your announcement, our stock was trading at thirty dollars a share. Since then it has dropped to nineteen dollars a share. At a loss of eleven dollars a share, the public value of the Koldex Corporation has dropped by almost" - his voice increased in intensity - "two hundred million dollars!"

Once again I was surprised. I had not had any idea, and felt a little foolish that I had not thought to check on the stock value of Koldex, but as I had told him, I just didn't follow the market. However, I did make a mental note to check on Belmont, and see what had happened to their stock since the press conference.

"Two hundred million dollars," he said again for emphasis. "Now you must understand that we cannot possibly make an offer until we have physically inspected the cave. There is no possible way to put a value on your company until we have physically seen this substance, and until we know how much of it is available, so let's stop the nonsense and determine how soon we can go through the cave."

"We have set the date for next Tuesday, and that is still on schedule. For your information, we estimate the total number of doses at about five million, and as you know from the test reports I sent you, it takes two doses per treatment. However, it appears that the substance regenerates itself rather quickly."

"Really?" he said.

"Yes, and you'll be able to observe that when someone visits the cave. We would expect your offer to be made on the basis of a per piece value, so if we can't deliver, for any reason, you have no financial responsibility to us. We would like to have your offer in our office a week from next Tuesday."

Jennie walked in my office and I pointed at a chair.

"My assistant is here, Mr. Gunderson, I am going to put you on the speaker phone."

"Very well. Next Tuesday is not very much time."

"Mr. Gunderson, if you are really serious about Cavernite, I believe that you can have a preliminary offer ready by that date. You could probably have a preliminary offer ready in a couple of days. "

He thought about that for a moment. "Very well. I will have an offer into your office by that date," Gunderson said. "However, I expect to have the opportunity to further discuss this situation with you before you accept any other offer, in the event that there would be any others. I hope you fully understand that."

"I believe I can agree to that, Mr. Gunderson. Who will be coming down to inspect the cave?"

"I will," he said.

I raised my eyebrows. "Out of curiosity, Mr. Gunderson, I believe I asked you if you had ever been down in a cave?"

"I told you, once when I was a small child."

"Well, as I told you, Mr. Gunderson, there are parts of this cave that are extremely narrow, and you are a very large man, Mr. Gunderson. Having personally been down in there, it is my opinion that it would be quite difficult, perhaps even impossible, for you to get through some of the tight areas. I would suggest that you designate someone else."

He thought about that for a moment. "Very well, I will send Mr. Gino Moretti. But I will probably accompany him to the farm." I had the feeling that for some reason he wanted to see the location in person. I was not pleased to hear that Moretti would be coming to the cave.

"We will meet you at the farmhouse at nine o'clock next Tuesday morning." His voice raised in intensity. "Remember, Mr. McCarthy, I intend to buy your company, and I warn you, do not accept an offer from anyone else. That concludes our business for today.

Jennie spoke first. "I believe that is one of the most intimidating, most evil men I've ever met in my life." She shuddered.

I nodded. "Yeah, he's pretty heavy, although I wonder just how much of that is for real and how much of it is for effect."

Jennie said, "I don't know how we could ever do business with a man like that, but on the other hand I wonder what he might do if we don't. He was dead serious about buying the company. He scares me, Brian. I'll admit it."

"Come on, Jennie. We live in a nation of laws. We can make whatever decision we want regarding Cavernite. Besides we don't even know what kind of an offer we're going to get from him, or whether we will even get one from Belmont after we talk to them tomorrow."

"Well, to quote the old expression," Jennie said, "it sounds to me like you're going to get an offer from Gunderson that you can't refuse. But I must say that you handled that very well, Brian. I'm not sure that I could have."

I smiled, but under the circumstances I didn't think Jennie's remark about "an offer you can't refuse" was all that funny.

"Quite honestly, though, I didn't know that the Cavernite announcement had brought his stock down that much," I said. "We need to find out what effect we've had on the Belmont stock before we talk to them today. Anyone know a broker?"

"Yeah, I've got one," Paul said. "I'll give him a call now, and find out what's going on."

As soon as we were through eating lunch, we headed over to Belmont. Was this going to be a repeat of the Koldex meeting?

Chapter Seventeen

P aul got on the phone with a broker he knew and found out that the Belmont stock hadn't been affected all that much, dropping down only a couple of points, from forty-three to forty-one. As I had mentioned before, Belmont was much larger than Koldex, and more diversified, so they wouldn't be nearly as affected by Cavernite coming on the market as Koldex would be. No wonder Gunderson was so adamant about buying the company.

The more I thought about that, and the more I thought about Gunderson himself, the more concerned I became about the security, or the lack of it, that we had down at the cave. I decided to call Vince Fernandez, the guy who had trained me in the Navy, and who was living on his avocado ranch in Fallbrook, a few miles north of San Diego.

I got his phone number out of my file and dialed it. That familiar voice came on the phone.

"Fernandez here."

"Hey, Vince, Brian McCarthy."

"McCarthy! How the hell are you?"

"Not bad, Vince. How's everything with you?"

"Well, its been a lousy year for avocados, but other than that everything else is O.K. So what have you been up to?"

Vince always liked to bitch about the avocado business, but if he ever decided to sell the acreage he had, he'd never have to worry about a thing the rest of his life. The land values had boomed in Fallbrook since he had bought the place.

"Well, let's see, Vince. I guess you know I got married."

"Yeah, poor girl. I'd like to meet her some time."

"Well, hopefully you will. Soon. Vince, I'm involved in something that's starting to make me a little nervous. I'd like to talk to you about it, and see if you've got some ideas."

"Sure, Brian, how can I help?"

"I don't want to talk about it on the phone, Vince. Why don't I drive down Saturday morning. You going to be around?"

"You bet. Come on down."

"Great. I'll see you then. And I'll bring Jennie along."

"Good idea. We'd love to meet her."

I felt better just talking to Vince. He had worked for a security company for a few years after he left the Navy, before he bought the ranch and moved to Fallbrook, so he could probably give me some good advice on what we could do to protect the cave.

I called Jim Adair, to make sure that he would be available next Tuesday.

"Jim? Brian McCarthy."

"Hello Brian. How you doin'?"

"Just fine, Jim. I'm coming down next Monday, and then Tuesday I have some people I'd like to take into the cave to look at the stuff. Are you going to be around?"

"I reckon so. How many people you wanna take down there?"

"Just a couple in the morning, let's say about nine o'clock, and then probably a couple more in the afternoon, about two o'clock, so it'll take the whole day."

"Sure, we can do that."

"Great. I'll see you Tuesday. Also I'm bringing a friend along with me, an old service buddy. We may want to talk about some more security for the cave."

"All right, Brian. We'll see you out at the farm on Tuesday mornin'."

I hung up the phone and looked at Jennie. "How would you like to go down in the cave Tuesday morning with the guy from Koldex?"

She smiled. "Hey, I'd really like to do that. Are you going in too?"

"I think so. I want to see if I can get an old buddy of mine, Vince Fernandez, to go along with us. If he's there he can keep an eye on Gunderson. I don't want Hugo wandering around by himself."

Jennie frowned. "Oh, that's right. That awful man is going to be down there too, isn't he?"

"Why Jennie. If I didn't know better, I'd think you didn't care for Hugo."

She shuddered involuntarily. "What a terrible man. I hate the thought of being around him."

I walked over to her and took her in my arms. "Don't worry about him."

✳✳✳

After lunch we headed over to our meeting with Belmont. They were located in a large new building out on Wilshire Boulevard. The directory in the lobby told us that their executive offices were on the twentieth floor.

We took the elevator up, announced ourselves to the receptionist, and spent the next few minutes browsing around the lobby, looking at displays of some of Belmont's products. It was quite a line of products, many of which I immediately recognized.

A woman appeared through a door, looked at us, and said, "Mr. McCarthy?"

"I'm Brian McCarthy, " I replied.

"I'm Marla O'Connor, Mr. Harrison's assistant. We talked on the phone." She extended her hand.

"Nice to meet to you. These are my associates, Jennie McCarthy, and Paul Miller." Everyone shook hands.

"Let me take you to Mr. Harrison's office." The tone of her voice was pleasant, but not warm, sort of clipped. Marla O'Conner was very professional, in her manner, in her dress and in her speech.

We were led into a large corner office, with a magnificent view of downtown Los Angeles. The decor of the office was very warm and pleasant, with some interesting looking paintings on the walls, which I guessed might be originals, and several plants were scattered around the room. I couldn't help but contrast the atmosphere here with the cold, impersonal feeling at Koldex.

Two men were sitting at a round table, and got up as we entered the room. I recognized James Harrison from the pictures I had seen of him, and he walked toward us. "Mr. McCarthy?"

"I'm Brian McCarthy," I said.

"Jim Harrison," he replied, and we went through the introduction and hand shaking routine again. The other man was introduced as Hugh Fleming, executive vice president of Belmont.

As we all sat down at the table, Harrison smiled. "Can I get you some coffee or anything?" There was a decanter on the table, together with cups, sugar and cream.

"Yes, thank you," I said, and he poured three cups of coffee.

He turned to his assistant. "Marla, would you hold all my calls, please."

Harrison started the meeting by saying, "Well, Brian, we're interested in learning more about this mysterious substance that you announced in New York last month. You've attracted a lot of attention in our industry."

"I guess that was the idea," I said. "You received the lab reports I sent you?"

"Yes, we did. Thank you. We have circulated them to several members of our staff. We're familiar with the organizations that did the testing, and I must say we were impressed, particularly with the patient testing."

" Actually," I smiled at Jennie, "Jennie was the first patient, sort of by accident. But the results we have had with the formal patient testing so far have been spectacular. We don't think there is much doubt about the validity and effectiveness of Cavernite."

"Based on what we know so far, that would appear to be the case," he said. "Tell us what your interest is in Belmont."

"Well, to start with, I'm an advertising guy," I nodded at Jennie and Paul, "and we run our own ad agency here in Los Angeles. Cavernite is something that I stumbled onto totally by chance, and I can give you more detail on how that happened later on, if we get to that point. But frankly, I don't have the time, the background or the resources to take the product to market, so I'm interested in finding someone who wants to do that. We are talking to a limited number of companies, and Belmont, as you very well know, is one of the leaders in the cold remedy business."

"Yes, you're correct." He paused. "Are you also talking to Koldex?"

"As a matter of fact, we have had a meeting with Hugo Gunderson."

He glanced over at Hugh Fleming, who said, "That must have been an interesting experience."

"It was probably an experience that none of us will forget very soon."

Jennie looked at Harrison. "Do you know him?" she asked.

"No," he said, "I have never had the pleasure of meeting Mr. Gunderson personally, but I understand he is sort of a unique character, kind of a legend in the industry." He looked at Fleming again. "Is legend the right word, Hugh?"

Fleming laughed. "I suppose it will do."

"I presume you would like to visit the location where Cavernite is growing?" I asked.

"Definitely," Harrison replied. "That would be a necessary step before we could start any sort of negotiation."

"Fine. We are prepared to do that. Actually Cavernite, as the name implies, was discovered in a cave. Are you aware of the location?"

Harrison frowned. "No, I'm not. Should I be?"

"Not necessarily. I was just curious. Anyway, the cave is a few miles from a small town called Cave Junction in the southern part of Kentucky. We are going to be down there next week, and could take some one from your company through the cave next Tuesday afternoon. Would that date be O.K.?"

The two men looked at each other. Hugh Fleming nodded. "I could make it down there next Tuesday, Jim. And it would probably be a good idea to take someone along from the lab."

I thought about the conversation with Gunderson. "We're going to be crawling through some pretty tight spots at times, Hugh, so you don't want to bring anyone down with you who is overweight, or who has any kind of problem with closed in spaces. I have a couple of experienced cavers who will take us in, but we really shouldn't take more than two of your people."

"Cavers?"

"Professional cave explorers."

"You've been down there?" Harrison asked.

I nodded. "Yeah, that's kind of how this stuff got discovered. I'll tell you the rest of the story some time." I already had the feeling that we might be doing business with Jim Harrison and Belmont, provided that their offer was fair.

"Anyway, We are asking a limited number of interested companies to submit a preliminary proposal to us by a week from Tuesday, outlining the basis on which you would like to proceed, if you are so inclined."

"That's pretty quick." Harrison shook his head. "I don't think we can move that fast."

"I realize there are a lot of details to work out, Jim. You are going to want to examine Cavernite carefully, and we know that there is still a lot of work to do to get final FDA approval. We've done some of it, as you've seen from the reports, but we would like for the company that is going to market the product to finish up the testing and whatever else is needed."

"Well, as you're beginning to find out, the drug business is pretty complicated, and the FDA can be very difficult to deal with."

"I know. I just don't want to spend any more time or money on this, and your people are a lot more familiar with the FDA and their procedures than we are. We've already got over a hundred thousand dollars invested in this project, and I'd like to get that back up front from whoever is going to handle the product."

We were being pretty candid with one another, in contrast with the fencing we had done with Gunderson.

"I imagine that Hugo Gunderson is interested," Harrison said. "I presume you're aware of the effect that your announcement had on his stock?"

"Yes, he pointed that out to us, rather forcefully, in fact."

"Rather forcefully," Jennie said.

"Jim, your stock only went down a point or so. what I think we would like to do is to simply agree on a contract to sell Cavernite to someone on a exclusive basis, probably on a per piece basis. That way you do not have a financial obligation to us unless we can deliver, and you aren't going to want to buy the stuff unless this product really does what we say it does, and until you get the necessary government approvals."

"That seems like it might work, but we'll have to study this very carefully. Hugh? Any comments?"

"Not really, Jim, although a week seems like it is a little fast to put together a proposal," he said.

"We're not looking for a final proposal," I said. "Just an outline of how we would work together, and what the value of Cavernite would be to you. I am sure that all of this will take some further discussion." It was interesting to me how reasonable I was willing to be with these people, and how unreasonable I had wanted to be with Gunderson.

"All right," Fleming said. "Give me some directions on how to get there, and I'll round up one of our skinnier lab people who doesn't suffer from claustrophobia."

We agreed to meet at the farm at two o'clock Tuesday afternoon, figuring that Gunderson should be out of there by then. I gave them directions on how to get there, and some idea of the clothing they should bring, something I had forgotten to do with Gunderson.

J. P. called early the next morning.

"Hello, Brian. I was just wondering how your meetings progressed?"

"I would say that they both went pretty well, J. P., although they certainly were different. Hugo Gunderson is everything they say he is."

"Yes, I imagine that was quite fascinating. Any thoughts at this point as to which way you will go?"

I decided to play it cool. I was still wondering how Gunderson had found out where the cave was, and the thought had occurred to me that we might have let something slip around J. P. I wasn't really being suspicious, just being cautious, or maybe paranoid.

"No, not really. It's much too early. They are both coming down to look over the cave next Tuesday, and then we'll see what happens after that."

"Would you like me to accompany you?"

"No, I don't think so."

"Hm. There doesn't seem to be a great deal for me to do at the moment, Brian, and I would like to continue to be of assistance to you, if possible."

"Well, I guess there really isn't much you can do right now, J. P. You've been very helpful to me in getting this thing off the ground, and I appreciate that, but we are just at a different stage now, and the fact is, there isn't much for any of us to do right now."

"I suppose that's true. Well, I'll stay in touch."

"O.K. Thanks, J. P."

I think he did feel left out of things, but what I said was right. There really wasn't anything for him to do now, and as far as our negotiations with the two companies were concerned, I didn't want to involve any outsiders.

***

Jennie and I drove down to Vince's ranch on Saturday. He had a great house, all adobe walls, with a red tile roof, very Spanish looking, and sitting up on top of a hill with a spectacular view of the avocado orchards and mountains. He and his wife Maria came out of the house as we parked the car. Vince looked great. He was tan and thin, had a big grin on that craggy, rugged face of his, and obviously was taking good care of himself. Maria was really nice, fat as a butterball, and they had raised two terrific boys, both out of college and doing well.

After I introduced them to Jennie, he just shook his head. "You must be crazy, lady, a beautiful girl like you getting mixed up with a no good Irishman like McCarthy."

"Oh stop it Vince," Maria said, giving me a kiss. "Can you two stay for lunch?"

"I don't know," I said. "What are you cooking?"

"For you, I think I'll make some enchiladas."

"Then we're staying." I looked at Jennie. We both loved Mexican food. "You haven't eaten enchiladas until you've tried Maria's."

"Sounds great," Jennie said.

The girls went inside together, and Vince and I walked down the hill toward the orchards.

"What's up?" he asked.

I gave him a general background on the recent events, including inheriting the farm, finding the cave, and then discovering Cavernite.

"I'm talking to a couple of pharmaceutical companies about buying this stuff, Vince, and frankly, the guy that runs one of them scares the hell out of me. I have the idea that he's capable of doing almost anything if he doesn't get his way. And he's made it clear that he intends to buy the business from us, whether we want to sell it to him or not. Our announcement knocked his stock way down, and he's obviously wounded."

I described our meeting with Hugo Gunderson, adding the information we had picked up on his reputation prior to that.

"I'll tell you, Vince. We haven't told anyone about the location of the cave, but he already knew where it was. That blew me away."

"Yeah, he sounds like a mean mother. What do you want me to do?"

"Well, I've had a gate put on the cave, but I don't think that would keep anyone out for very long who really wanted to get inside. What I'd like for you to do is go down with me next week, take a look around, and give me some suggestions on security. By the way, this is a business deal, so I want to pay for your time and expenses. I'm hiring you as a security consultant."

"Hey, no way man. I don't want to do that. We're buddies."

"Look, Vince. There are big bucks involved in this deal, maybe millions a year, so there's no reason why I shouldn't pay for your time."

"Well, we'll talk about it."

"Don't fight me, Vince. I really need your help. By the way, this guy Gunderson is going to be down there Tuesday, so you'll get a chance to meet him. He's too big to take through parts of the cave, and I don't want him wandering around by himself, so maybe you can keep an eye on him for me while we're down in there with his guy."

"Sure thing," Vince said. "I'd like to meet him."

"I want you to. I've got a bad feeling about having him down there. He knows he can't go into the cave, but he's still coming down. I don't like it."

Then we walked back up to the house for lunch, and the world's greatest enchiladas.

Chapter Eighteen

ennie, Vince and I got down to the farm late Monday afternoon, and it was already getting dark, so Vince didn't have much of a chance to look around. It was pretty cold there, and the house was chilly when we opened it up, so we threw some logs in the fireplaces, and the place warmed up in a hurry. We put Vince in the spare bedroom.

The next morning Jim Adair showed up around eight-thirty. Will Johnson was with him, and they had brought along enough gear, stacked on the back of the pick-up truck, to take six people into the cave.

We shook hands. "Jim Adair, this is Vince Fernandez, an old buddy of mine from the Navy. Among other things, Vince is an expert on security, so I want him to take a look around, and make some suggestions. Frankly, I'm a little concerned about the wrong people getting into the cave."

Jim nodded. "Pleased to meet you." He looked at me. "You want me to take him through the cave?"

I looked at Vince, who shook his head, pretty emphatically. "No, I don't think that will be necessary. I'm more interested in the area outside the cave. Besides, I guess I've got a little touch of claustrophobia, so I'd just as soon stay out of there."

"Is that right, Vince?" I asked. "As I recall, you were in some pretty tight spots back in the old days."

"Yeah," he said. "That's probably where it came from."

"Well, in that case you can keep an eye on Gunderson for me while we're down in the cave. By the way, Jim, I would like for Jennie to see the room where the Cavernite is growing and the big room where all of the stalagmites are. Is it O.K. if she goes down with us?"

"Sure, Brian. Be my pleasure." He smiled at Jennie. "How's the ankle doing?" He glanced back at me briefly, as if to acknowledge that I wasn't totally off the hook yet for that foolishness.

"Just doing fine, Jim," Jennie said.

At that point a black Cadillac came up the driveway and stopped near the house. We watched as Hugo Gunderson unfolded out of the back seat, dressed again in a black suit, grey shirt, bright red tie and sun glasses. That seemed to be standard uniform for him. Both Jim and Vince just stared at him for a minute. Jennie looked troubled.

Jim turned to me and said in a low voice. "That fella ain't plannin' on going down in the cave, is he?"

I had to keep from laughing. "No, Jim. He brought someone else along to go with you. I already told him he would have a problem down there."

"Problem, hell," Jim said. "He'd just plain get stuck down in there."

I walked over to Gunderson, while his driver got out of the other side of the car. We shook hands, and Gunderson said, "This is Gino Moretti."

Moretti was about my size, but stocky, with dark features and black, curly hair and sort of unsavory looking, like some gangsters I'd seen in movies. I nodded and we shook hand, and then I turned back to Gunderson. "I've seen Mr. Moretti before. A few weeks ago he followed me down to Kentucky."

Gunderson shrugged casually. "Is that so?"

"Yes, that's so. What does Mr. Moretti do in your organization?"

Gunderson looked at me coldly. "He's in administration."

Yeah, administration, I thought to myself, wondering what this guy would administer.

"He's going down in the cave?" I asked.

"If necessary," Gunderson said, "but I would prefer to go down myself."

Jim Adair spoke up, shaking his head, obviously unfazed by Gunderson. "I'm sorry mister, but they ain't no way you could get through the places we gotta get through. I just wouldn't take you down there."

I smiled innocently and shrugged. "When it comes to the cave, he's the boss."

Gunderson scowled. "Then I guess it'll have to be Mr. Moretti."

"All right." I turned to Moretti. "I guess I owe you an apology, Mr. Moretti. I should have said something to Mr. Gunderson about clothing for the cave. As we've said, there are going to be some pretty close quarters down where you're going, so I would suggest you take off your suit coat, and we'll lend you a sweater and knee pads."

Moretti said nothing, but looked at Gunderson, who nodded his head. I estimated the cost of the suit he was wearing at several hundred dollars.

"O.K. then," I said. "This is Jim Adair, who's going to lead us down into the cave, and this is Will Johnson, who will help him. Jim is an expert in cave exploration, and when we're down in the cave we do whatever he says, understood? He's the boss."

Adair said, "If you folks'll step over here to the truck, we'll show you a little bit about your gear."

All Jim really did was to show them how to use the carbide lamp, although he told them he didn't think it would be necessary for either Moretti or Jennie to use them. But he was always thorough, and wanted them to be somewhat familiar with the equipment.

After everyone got outfitted, the five of us proceeded back to the cave entrance, Gunderson and Vince Fernandez following behind. Jim unlocked the padlock on the gate and slid it open. He had given the emergency phone number to Vince, since Jennie was coming down with us. Vince also would be keeping an eye on Hugo Gunderson for me while we were down in the cave.

We progressed through the tunnel without incident, although I could see that the narrow ledge we had to cross made Moretti a little nervous. For that matter, it made me a little nervous too. Jim Adair led the way, with Will Johnson bringing up the rear. I could tell from his expression that Moretti was not real crazy about this whole thing, especially in the tight areas where we had to get down and crawl on our hands and knees. Jennie was doing fine, and we stopped for a few minutes in the first room to let her look around at some of the formations.

"That's amazing, Brian," she said.

"Wait until you see the big room down in the other tunnel."

Moretti said, "We gonna stay here all day?"

"We'll get there," I said. "Just hold your horses. Are you ready, Jennie?"

"Uh huh," she said, and we went on to the Cavernite room.

"Good Lord!" Jennie exclaimed when she first saw it. "It's really weird when you see a whole roomful of it, Brian."

Moretti looked casually around the room, not saying anything, and apparently not all that interested in what he was seeing. Then he pulled a metal tape measure out of his pocket.

"What are you doing?' I asked.

"Mr. Gunderson told me to measure the room," he replied in a husky voice.

I guess that's "O. K." I watched as he measured the length, width and height of the room. Moretti scribbled something on a piece of paper, which I presumed were the dimensions of the room. Then he put the tape measure away, and took a switchblade knife out of his pants pocket and opened it up.

"Now what are you doing?" I asked.

"Mr. Gunderson told me to get some samples while I was down here," he said.

I shook my head. "Sorry, no samples."

He glared at me, raising his voice. "Mr. Gunderson told me to bring back some samples."

"Mr. Moretti, I don't give a damn what Mr. Gunderson told you. It's my cave, not Mr. Gunderson's. No samples."

"Mr. Gunderson said he's going to buy the cave."

"Well, he may or he may not, but he hasn't bought it yet, so no samples. Are you all ready to go back?" I asked, anxious to get Moretti out of there.

Moretti ran his thumb slowly over the sharp edge of the knife, smiled at me, and then put it away, although I think he would just as soon have cut my throat with it. We got back out to the entrance, and looking at my watch, it had been about an hour and forty-five minutes since we had gone in.

When we got back near the house, Moretti went over to Gunderson, who was standing next to their car, gave him the piece of paper he had written the measurements on, and then said something to him quietly that we couldn't hear. I was looking at Moretti's pants, which were a wreck. I didn't think that a dry cleaner was going to be able to clean up that mess, which was not something I was going to lose a lot of sleep over.

Gunderson whirled around and walked over to where I was standing with the rest of the group. He hissed, "I told Moretti to bring me back some samples!" I was getting the idea that the angrier that Gunderson got, the more he hissed, sort of like a snake.

"First of all, we haven't agreed to furnish samples to you yet, Mr. Gunderson. In fact, we haven't even discussed it. And secondly, even if you did bring some out, they would have to be maintained at the same temperature that they grow in down in the cave. I don't believe you have any way to do that, do you?"

"No, I don't." He glared at all of us for a moment. "Very well. You will have my offer a week from today, Mr. McCarthy. I will talk to you after that and we will conclude our arrangement. Do you understand?"

I stood my ground and glared back at him. "We'll look forward to taking a look at it."

"Let's go," he said to Moretti. They both got in the car, Moretti in the driver's seat, Gunderson climbing in the back seat alone, and Moretti sped off down the driveway, churning gravel and creating a cloud of dust.

I looked at the other three. Jim Adair spoke first, shaking his head. "That sure does seem like one mean fella, Brian."

I nodded. "Yeah, so is the other guy, but Gunderson's the reason I am worried about security. What did he do while we were down in the cave, Vince?"

"Oh, he wandered around a little bit, just sort of looking around. He didn't talk to me at all, but I got the feeling that he was taking in almost everything that he wanted to. Actually, he spent most of the time in the car on the telephone. I can see why you're concerned about him, though. He seems like a nasty son of a bitch."

"Well, you know how I feel about him, Brian," Jennie added.

"Yeah, I sure do, babe. I'll tell you what, Jennie, if you and Jim could go get us some sandwiches for lunch, I'll take Vince for a tour around the grounds before the Belmont people arrive, O.K.?"

"Sure."

After they left, Vince and I walked back toward the cave again, proceeding slowly along the creek as Vince looked over the area. When we got fairly near the cave entrance we cut up a hill to the right, putting us in an area that would probably be over the cave itself. This part of the farm was pretty rocky, with some trees scattered through it, and obviously not much good for farming.

"How far back does your property go?" Vince asked.

"Several hundred feet. It runs into another farm back there," I pointed, "but there aren't any roads in that area."

"But someone could get on your property from that direction if they wanted to, right?"

"Oh, sure they could."

"O.K.," he nodded. "Let's head on back."

When we got back to the house, I asked, "Well, what do you think, Vince."

He grimaced. "It's a tough one, Brian. We could always put in some trip wires or traps that would set off some either some lights or flares or alarms, you know, stuff like that. The problem is, you're out in the country where someone could come at the cave from any direction. Also, I imagine there's a certain amount of wildlife around here that could accidentally set the alarms off, so that could get to be a real nuisance. And even if we did set up some alarms, there's no one out here on the property to respond to them anyway."

"Yeah, I see what you mean."

"One solution would be to put some guards out here, and tighten up the security around the cave entrance itself. But I've got to tell you, that would really be expensive."

I shook my head. "I'm not sure whether we could even find people to hire as guards around here, Vince."

He nodded. "I know. Maybe Jim Adair could give us some ideas on that, but remember, you're talking a lot of bucks. For two guards around the clock, seven days a week, you're looking at a minimum of ten thousand dollars a month. You'd almost have to have two of them, because I don't think one guard's going to do you much good. Not against someone who really wants to get in there."

I gulped and shook my head. "That kind of money just isn't in the cards, Vince."

"Yeah, I understand. Tell me what you're trying to do, Brian. Is it to keep people out of there, so they won't get hurt, or is it to protect the stuff down in the cave, or what?"

"Well, mainly I just want to make sure that no one gets in and messes around with the Cavernite."

"O.K., then. What we ought to do is figure out how we can stop anyone from going down into the cave. That might be easier."

"Good. I'll have Jim take you part way into the entrance of the cave, so you can at least see what it's like, and then maybe you can give me some ideas."

Jim took him in the cave right after lunch, and although Vince didn't go in very far, he came out looking shaky.

"Man, that really gets to me," he said, shaking his head. "I'll be happy to be your consultant, Brian, but somebody else is going to have to do the work. There's no way I could stay in there for any length of time."

Hugh Fleming from Belmont showed up a few minutes before two o'clock, with another man from his company. They had brought some old clothes along, at my suggestion, and went in the house to change. Then we put them through the abbreviated training session, and started back down into the cave again. Jennie stayed behind with Vince this time.

When we got back to the room, their technical man was obviously fascinated by the Cavernite, and spent some time examining it. He pointed at the spot where it was growing back.

"It appears that it is regenerating itself here. Had you cut some off?"

"Exactly," I said. "And it seems to grow back pretty fast. We cut the first samples about six months ago, and the new ones are almost completely grown out again." I pointed at an area on the wall. "I cut some of the new ones here, and they're coming back again. Apparently they only get so big."

"I wonder if the new ones will have the same effectiveness?" Hugh asked.

"I don't know, Hugh. I guess that's something you'll have to test."

"Do you mind if I cut some off?" Hugh asked.

"Well, I would prefer that you didn't. Besides, you don't have any way of maintaining it at the cave temperature, so it wouldn't do you much good. We can furnish you samples later on."

"O.K." he said.

When we got back out, Hugh Fleming said, "That's pretty amazing, Brian. It looks like Cavernite is for real, and I know we're going to be anxious to test the new growth as soon as possible, that is, if we get involved with you. I'll talk to Jim Harrison tomorrow, and we should be able to have a preliminary offer to you by next Tuesday."

We watched as they drove down to the highway. "Nice people," Vince said.

"Yes, they are," Jennie said. "And it looks like they are genuinely interested in putting Cavernite on the market."

Vince looked at me. "I guess you're going to have to decide which group you want to do business with."

"Yeah, but unless there's a big difference in the offers, I think we've already pretty well decided."

"Well, as a suggestion, Brian, if you do decide to go with these people, I'd delay telling Gunderson that for as long as you can. At least until we can get some security set up around here."

"Good idea, Vince. I will. Whatever we decide, we'll keep it strictly to ourselves as long as we can. When will I hear back from you?"

"I want to think about it a little, but I should be able to call you in a couple of days. Then we can talk about what to do and how to get it done."

I turned to Jim Adair. "We've got a late evening flight back to the coast, so we'd better get on the road. Thanks again for your help, Jim. I appreciate it."

"Always a pleasure, Brian. Pleased to meet you Vince. Bye, Jennie. See you all soon."

We were on our way back home, and although I found myself worrying about Gunderson, I kept my thoughts to myself.

Chapter Nineteen

The following Tuesday we received Federal Express packages from both Koldex and Belmont. I opened them up, and saw that both envelopes contained the offers we were waiting for. I made two copies of each of the documents, and sat down to go over them with Paul and Jennie.

Before I gave them the copies. I said, "All right, folks, I just want to make one thing clear, just for the record. Nothing we're going to talk about here is to be discussed with anyone else. Anyone. I am very concerned about security, particularly because of Hugo Gunderson. Should we decide to accept an offer from Belmont, I want to delay giving Gunderson that news until the last possible moment. O.K.?" The speech was really for Paul's benefit. Jennie already knew what the score was.

They both nodded agreement, and we started reading.

I started with the Koldex offer, which was seventy-five cents per piece. It was based on exclusive rights to Cavernite, and there were no other conditions other than one that stipulated that both parties were bound to the contract for a period of twenty years.

There was a second paragraph stating that, in addition to the contract for Cavernite, McCarthy Communications would be appointed as the advertising agency for Koldex for a three-year period. The offer also estimated current billings at twenty million dollars a year. That was an interesting twist.

Then I went through the Belmont offer. First of all, they said they would buy Cavernite, again on an exclusive basis, at fifty cents per piece. They also guaranteed that they would buy a minimum of three million pieces a year, so long as we could supply them. The contract was for a five-year period, renewable by either party for an additional five year period. They also would reimburse us for our up front costs, up to one hundred thousand dollars, which was important to me.

However, there were conditions on the Belmont offer. The first was that Cavernite would get approval by the FDA, secondly that the new growth would be as effective as the original growth, and finally that there was no major problem with shelf life after Cavernite was shipped to pharmacies.

They also said that they would build a storage facility on the farm, and would either be responsible for cutting and removing the product, or would accept delivery after we had done that, whichever we preferred.

I waited until we were all through reading the offers. "Well?"

Jennie spoke first. "Obviously, the Koldex offer is better, at least on the surface, Brian. But I get the feeling that what he really wants is control. If we signed with him, we're tied up for twenty years, and there's no guarantee that he'll buy any quantity from us at all, like there is in the Belmont offer. So, if Gunderson doesn't put it on the market, there wouldn't be a thing we could do about it. And that may be just what he wants to do."

I nodded. "Good point, Jennie. I saw that myself. He may just be looking for a way to tie us up. By the way, any final agreement will have to be reviewed by our lawyer. Paul? Any thoughts?"

"Well, just looking at Koldex, we'd have to see if we couldn't deal with some of those problems, like getting a guarantee of the amount of advertising they will approve each year.

"Not if the client doesn't want to cooperate, Paul," she said, standing up. "You know as well as I do that a client can create a situation where it's impossible to work with them. Ads don't get approved, schedules lag, all the usual things. And if ads don't get placed, there's no commission!"

"I know that, Jennie," Paul said, "but Koldex also needs to sell so many pieces per year, and they'll have to advertise aggressively to do that. However, from the agency's point of view, it is a very attractive offer, Brian. It would really increase our billing, and would put the agency on a whole different level. We'd be buying consumer media on a national basis, and, of course, we would have to staff up to handle the business. Fifteen percent of twenty million is three million bucks a year in media commissions."

Jennie came right back. "How much after taxes, and they don't have to advertise to sell anything if they don't buy them from us in the first place."

"Well it looks to me like we take the Koldex offer." I said.

"What?" Jennie said. "You've got to be kidding."

I laughed. "Calm down, Jennie. I was just kidding."

"Well it's not very funny." she replied.

I told her about his offer, including the stock options, and that he was going to call back tomorrow for an answer. I could see that we were getting two different points of view here. Paul was looking at it more from the agency side, which was understandable, since he had little to gain from the sale of Cavernite. On the other hand, Jennie was looking at it more from the Cavernite point of view. Besides which, she didn't want to do business with Gunderson anyway.

"Yes, but I wonder just how long Gunderson would honor the advertising contract," she responded, "and how tough he would be to work with."

"Hey, a contract's a contract." Paul said.

They were both getting pretty emotional.

"Koldex needs to advertise to stay competitive, so they have some strong incentives on their side as well."

"I don't think it would bother Gunderson if he had to stop advertising for a while," Jennie said. She was bristling now. "Not if he had to do it to get his way. I just don't trust him. You were there in his office. The man's an animal!"

"Hold on, everybody!" I said. "Let's calm down and get back to the offers. What about Belmont?"

"Well, its lower than Koldex's," Jennie said, sitting back down, "but it's probably just an opening offer, and I think we can get them to go higher. However, it does have a guaranteed minimum, and they will pay us back our expenses just for signing. It's also a much more business-like approach. They've thought about things like the new growth and shelf life, and I think that means they are serious about putting Cavernite on the market. Koldex sure as hell isn't!"

"Paul?"

"Well, Jennie's right. It is a first offer. It is for both companies, and we can probably get them to go higher. I guess what we have to do is to decide whether we want to pick one company to negotiate with or both of them. You haven't told us what you think about this, Brian."

"First of all, I think we should negotiate with both of them, even if it's Belmont that we want to do business with. I don't want Gunderson to think that he's out of the picture, and the higher he goes, the more leverage we have with Belmont anyway. We ought to get the best deal we can."

"I'll bet we can get Belmont up to a dollar a piece. Maybe more," Jennie said.

We kicked this back and forth for another half hour or so, and finally concluded that we wanted a dollar a piece, a minimum of a three million piece guarantee per year, and our up front expenses reimbursed. We also decided that it would be better if the winner took full charge of all phases of production, but that we would have the right to audit the process. I knew that Jennie and I were leaning strongly toward Belmont, but Paul wanted us to negotiate seriously with Koldex. The advertising aspect of their offer was still very much on his mind.

"I'll be frank with you, Paul. I understand your feelings about getting the Koldex ad account, but no matter which way it goes, there will be money to pump into the shop."

"Yeah, if you don't retire." He said it with a smile but the message was there. "Look, I can understand how you feel about Gunderson, Brian. I met the guy. But his offer sure is tempting, at least to me.

What if you mentioned the advertising deal to Belmont? Maybe they're already unhappy with their agency. You never know."

"Who is their agency," I asked.

"I don't know," he said, "but I'll find out."

"O. K. I'll mention it to Jim Harrison and see what he says."

We broke up the meeting and I called Harrison, but got Marla O'Conner on the line instead.

"Good afternoon, Mr. McCarthy. Mr. Harrison is out of the office today. Can I help you?"

"Yes, you can. Tell him that we received your offer, and I would like to talk to him about it."

"He'll be in the office tomorrow, and I'll have him call you. Is there anything you would like for me to pass on to him?"

"No, I don't think so."

"Could I tell him that the offer was satisfactory?" She was pushing, which seemed a little strange, since she hadn't sat in on our meeting.

"Just tell him that we need to discuss it."

"Very well. I'll have him call you."

I hung up, still thinking about the conversation with Marla, which struck me as a little strange.

Jim Harrison called early the next morning, on Wednesday.

"Good morning, Brian. How are you?"

"Just fine, Jim. And you?"

"Good, thank you. Marla tells me that you received our offer."

"Yes I did."

"I've got Hugh here in the office with me. I'm going to put you on the speaker phone, O.K.?"

"That's fine. I think I'll get Jennie in here as well, and do the same thing."

Once we got everything set, Harrison continued.

"Well, I must tell you that Hugh was very impressed by what he saw down at the cave last week."

"That's right," Hugh said.

"Yeah, I'm glad he was able to come down. Let me tell where we are, Jim, and I'm going to be up front with you, because we'd prefer to make a deal with you if we can, O.K.?"

"Great. We'll be just as up front with you, Brian. It's the way we do business."

"As you know, we are also talking to Koldex."

"O.K."

"Well, the bottom line is that you're low. Gunderson came in at seventy-five cents. We've discussed it here, and what we would like from you is a dollar fifty a piece. I know Gunderson would go that high, maybe higher, but we'll settle for that. Everything else is fine, and we'd like you to handle all aspects of the production of the product, but we'd like to have the right to inspect and audit."

There was a pause on the other end of the line. "I don't know, Brian. We would really have to take a hard look at the pricing. There will be a lot of expenses involved in getting a new product like this off the ground."

"Look, Jim. This product is going to be a sensation. Besides that, you have no development or manufacturing costs, which would ordinarily cost you millions. I don't know what you are planning on selling Cavernite for, but people will be willing to pay a lot to get rid of a cold overnight. And besides that, you have no competition."

"Well, we're going to have to talk this over, Brian. Was there anything else?"

"No, everything else in your offer was fine, but there is one other thing I'd like to talk to you about. One of the provisions in the Koldex offer was that they would give us a three-year contract to handle their advertising account, which is about twenty million dollars in billing a year. That was a very attractive part of their offer. Any thoughts on that?"

This time there was a long pause. Then Hugh Fleming came on the line.

"I guess that's my bailiwick, Brian, since I'm in charge of marketing around here. Frankly, we are very happy with our current agency, and wouldn't toss them out just to make this deal. It's not the way we operate. I hope that you, being in the advertising business yourself, you can appreciate that. I'm sure you've seen agencies lose accounts for the wrong reasons."

"I understand, Hugh, but it doesn't hurt to ask. When can you get back to us on the pricing?"

"We'll call you back later today or in the morning," Harrison said.

"O.K. We'll wait for your call." I hung up the phone.

"I suppose Paul will be disappointed if we end up with Belmont," Jennie said, "but I'll sure feel a lot better about it."

"Well, I can understand where he's coming from, but we really will be able to beef up the agency with the money from Cavernite, and I agree with you that handling Koldex's advertising would be a very shaky proposition."

A couple of hours later Harrison called back.

"Brian, we've talked it over, and we're willing to go to a dollar."

"A dollar? That's the best you can do?"

"Yes, it really is, Brian."

"Well," I winked at Jenny, "Right now we have an offer from your competitor for a dollar and a half. If you can match that now, I think we have a deal."

"I don't know, Brian, but we'll talk that over and get back to you."

"How soon can you get back to us. We'd really like to get this wrapped up."

"We'll call you back today."

I hung up the phone and looked at Jennie. "It doesn't hurt to try."

They called us back about two hours later. It was James Harrison.

"Brian? I'll tell you what. We've talked this over and the best we can do is a dollar and a quarter, and that's stretching it. If everything goes really well we might look at raising it a bit more later on. How's that?"

I thought to myself: an extra twenty-five cents times three million is seven hundred and fifty thousand dollars. Not bad.

"OK, Jim. You've got a deal. Send the paper work over here. But let's keep this quiet for the time being. I don't want Gunderson to find out about it. Not yet. How long do you think it will take to get it on the market?"

"I'm not sure off the top of my head. There's a lot to do, getting a new product out.

"Yeah, I've been dealing with the FDA out here, so I've got a pretty good idea about what's involved. By the way, you should be thinking about security for the cave. All that's protecting it now is a gate and a padlock."

"Good point, Brian. We'll take over the responsibility for the security as soon as you sign with us."

"I'd also suggest that we keep this as quiet as possible, just to be on the safe side. I won't indicate to Gunderson that we have a deal until we get the place secured. I'm really concerned about that."

"O.K. We'll move as quickly as we can on our end, and we'll keep it under wraps back here."

"Great. Talk to you soon."

I gave Jennie a big hug. "It looks like we've got a deal."

She grinned from ear to ear. "God, that's great, Brian!"

"Yeah. I think maybe we ought to keep this just between the two of us. I trust Paul, but for the time being, the fewer people who know the better. In the meantime, I'll stall Gunderson as long as I can."

The next morning, on Thursday, I got a call from Gunderson.

He started in quickly. "I haven't heard from you, Mr. McCarthy. I presume you received our offer?"

"Yes I did, Mr. Gunderson. We're looking it over."

"You've had two days." That sibilant quality was back in his voice. "Don't play games with me, Mr. McCarthy. It could be dangerous. Our offer is not that complicated. I presume it is satisfactory?"

My Irish temper was starting to rise, but I knew I had to stay cool. "Well, as a matter of fact, there are a couple of major problems with it."

"Such as what?"

"First of all, there's the price. We would like to see it at a dollar twenty-five. Secondly, we would like some kind of guaranteed purchase. As it is, you could tie us up for twenty years, and never buy a thing."

"I see. Very well then, I am willing to go to a dollar. As far as the guaranteed purchase, I cannot do that. There are too many unknowns with this product. However, I tell you what I will do. I will give you options on one hundred thousand shares of Koldex at the current market price, just for signing the agreement, As you know, it is down over ten dollars right now. As soon as we make the announcement on the contract with you, it will not only recover the ten dollars a share, but should go even higher. You will make over one million dollars, Mr. McCarthy. You could retire, travel around the world, do whatever you want to do. And your agency will have the Koldex account."

"That's very interesting, Mr. Gunderson. We will have to talk it over."

"Mr. McCarthy", His voice got louder. "Have you signed with Belmont?"

"No, we haven't", which was technically the truth.

"I think you're lying to me."

"Why do you say that?"

"Because I know." He hung up the phone.

I stuck my head in Jennie's office. "Our friend Gunderson just called. It's obvious he isn't going to take no for an answer, so I agreed to his offer."

She jumped up. "You what?"

"Relax, babe. Just a joke, but it won't be long before we hear from him again."

"I'm going out to lunch. I'll see you later."

It was about eleven-thirty Friday morning when Gunderson called. As usual he was right to the point.

"What is your answer, Mr. McCarthy?"

"Well, we're still thinking it over, Mr. Gunderson. I'm sure you must know that we are talking to other companies besides yours."

This time he really hissed at me. "I have warned you, Mr. McCarthy. It is dangerous to play games with me. Yes, I know that you are talking to Belmont. And I also know that my offer is better than theirs."

This startled me. "How would you know that?"

"I know many things, Mr. McCarthy. I want an answer from you. Or perhaps you have already accepted their offer."

This was really getting heavy. Gunderson was getting information from somewhere.

"Nothing is final yet. We hope to reach a decision next week. And of course, no matter what we decide, all final offers must be received here in writing, and will have to be reviewed by our lawyers and accountants. You know that."

"I think you are lying to me. Perhaps we will talk later on today." He said this in a strange tone, like he was baiting me or something. The phone went dead.

I didn't feel good at all about that conversation. I looked in Jennie's office, but she wasn't there. I went out to the reception desk.

"Have you seen Jennie?" I asked Patty, our receptionist.

"She went out to grab some lunch and run some errands, Brian. She said she'd be back by about one o'clock."

At two o'clock she still wasn't back, and nobody had heard from her. That wasn't like Jennie, and she always stayed in touch during the day, especially if her plans changed. I was starting to get worried.

I was also concerned about the last phone conversation I had with Gunderson. He seemed to have a lot of inside information. There had to be a leak somewhere. I didn't think it was at our end, so it almost had to be with Belmont. I was going to have to talk to James Harrison about this.

Then my dog Charlie came padding into my office.

"Hey, Charlie. Where's Jennie? We pay you a lot of money to be a guard dog." Charlie hopped up on the couch and went to sleep, a really impressive performance.

Chapter Twenty

J ennie finally showed up around two-thirty.

"Where in the Hell have you been," I demanded.

She gave me a big grin. "Well, since you are so nosey, I'll tell you. I went to see a doctor."

"Something wrong?"

"That all depends," she replied.

"What do you mean?"

"It depends on whether you would like to have a girl or a a boy."

"What?"

"Yes, dear. I'm pregnant."

"Oh, my God." I threw my arms around her. You're kidding me!"

"No, I'm not. I was at the OB's office today. I'm about two months pregnant. What would you like, a boy or a girl?"

"Have you put the order in yet?"

"Very funny. No, it's a little late for that."

"You know, I don't really care, Jennie, as long as the baby is healthy and it looks like you."

"Well, Brian, how does Mary McCarthy sound?"

"That's beautiful, Jennie. Just beautiful."

"A little baby girl."

"Then it has to look like you."

"We'll see, we'll see," she said.

"We're going out for a big dinner tonight to celebrate. Who else do you want to tell around here?"

"Nobody yet. Let's wait a little while. OK?"

"Sure. Whatever you want to do, babe."

Jennie went back to her office and I was sitting there, thinking about the news and how it would change our lives, when my phone rang. It was our receptionist.

"Brian, there are a couple of people here in the lobby to see you."

"Well, I don't have any appointments. Who are they?"

"It's a man and a woman. She says she's your ex-wife."

"Good Lord. Lila. What in the world would she want? Well, send 'em back."

Lila walked in a minute later, accompanied by a scruffy-looking middle-aged guy. It had been a few years since I had seen Lila, and frankly time hadn't been very kind to her. There were a lot of lines in her face and her hair was turning gray. She looked twenty years older.

"I'm busy, Lila. What can I do for you?"

"Plenty, Brian. I read in the paper where you struck it rich in some cave you own. Is that right."

"It's a little early to tell, Lila. But even if it's true it's no business of yours."

"Well, when we separated, I didn't get a thing from you. Now it is payback time."

"All that's water over the bridge, Lila. I don't owe you a thing."

The guy spoke up. "I'm Lila's fiance, and I'm here to see that she gets treated properly."

"Lila's fiance, eh. Well aren't you lucky. Let me tell you something, pal. She got treated properly when we divorced, and that was a long time ago. I don't owe her a thing. And anyway, she was screwing around with half the guys in Hollywood. Not that it did her any good."

He looked at me belligerently. "Well, I don't see it that way.

"Mister, whatever your name is, I don't really care how you see it. Now, I've got things to do, so why don't you two just run along."

He advanced toward me, his hands forming into two fists.

"Look," I warned him. "I spent my time in the Navy in special forces, learning how to take guys like you apart, so just get the Hell out of here before you get hurt." My Irish temper was flaring up.

He kept on coming and threw a right at me. It was pretty pathetic, and the next thing he knew he was lying on the floor, with his right arm twisted behind his back.

"OK, Bozo. You can go out of here one of two ways. One way is with your arm the way it is. The other way is with your arm broken."

I gave his arm an extra push upward.

"Ow," he yelled.

"Which way is it?"

"OK, OK. We'll leave."

I let go of his arm, but watched him carefully as he got up.

"You know where the door is, and take this tramp with you." I nodded at Lila.

"You'll be hearing from my lawyer," Lila said.

"Lila, any lawyer who would take your pathetic case ought to have his license revoked. Now get out of here."

Jennie was standing outside my door as they exited. When the door closed she looked quizzically at me.

"Who was that?"

"That, my dear, was my ex wife, somebody you don't want to meet."

"That was your ex?"

"Yeah, but she looked a lot better a few years ago. See what a life of sin does to you?"

"That must of been a lot of sin. By the way, Bob Wagner's here to talk about the press conference follow-up."

I glanced at my watch. "OK, let's meet in my office in twenty minutes. In the meantime I'll run up the street and get us some sandwiches."

"Want me to do it?" she said.

"Nah, I'll go. My car's right out in front."

I jumped in the car and started pulling out into the traffic, when I saw a car suddenly pulling out in front of me. I hit the brakes and absolutely nothing happened. I turned the wheel quickly and guided the car into a lamppost, destroying the grill, but avoiding the other car.

I got out of the car and slid underneath the front. I immediately saw where my brakes had been tampered with.

"Christ, what if I had been in heavy traffic. No telling what might have happened."

I stood there for a minute thinking about it. "OK, if Gunderson wants to play rough, I guess we can do that too."

I went back inside and explained to Jennie what had happened, then got on the phone to Vince Fernandez, I told him what I wanted to do, and he said he would be up by late afternoon.

All in all it had been a pretty interesting day. I became a father-to-be, and my car was disabled by somebody, probably by Gunderson, I wrecked my car, and oh yes, got to see my ex-wife. What else could happen?

The next day Jennie was late getting back from lunch again, and I was just starting to worry about her. Then one of the girls, Dottie Busher from creative, knocked on my door-frame. "Brian. Got a minute?"

"Sure, come on in, Dottie".

She seemed a little hesitant.

"Brian, I'm not sure this means anything, but I thought you ought to know."

"Know what?"

"Well, I was walking back to the office after lunch today, and Jennie was about a half block ahead of me."

"Yes?"

"And well, it seemed like, all of a sudden this big black limousine pulled up to the curb next to her."

"Go one." I didn't like what I was hearing.

"Then this man jumped out of the limo and grabbed Jennie."

"What?" I was getting nervous.

"It looked like she was trying to resist him, but he was bigger and stronger and he forced her into the back seat, and then the limo took off."

"Do you remember what he looked like?"

"I'm not sure, Brian, but I guess I'd describe him as sort of Italian, swarthy and kind of stocky, with all of this curly black hair."

That sounded like Gunderson's side-kick Moretti. My Irish temper was really up now. They had apparently kidnapped Jennie and there was no telling what those scum bags might do to her, and on top of that, she was pregnant. Somebody would pay for this.

Chapter Twenty-One

I called Vince Fernandez right away and ask him if he could drive up to the office as soon as possible. I told him what had happened to Jennie, and to my car, and that it was time for some serious talk about security. I described a plan I was thinking about, and said that we needed to talk about it. He said sure, he was leaving right now. Vince arrived late that afternoon and I filled him in on the recent events. He took a look at my brakes, and came back up shaking his head.

"Jesus, Brian, that could have been serious, depending on where you where."

"I guess in a way I was lucky, but I don't feel very charitable. That son-of-a-bitch Gunderson is the only person I can think of who had a reason to try something like that. Now it's our turn. Did you bring all the stuff we'll need?"

He nodded, pointing at a suitcase next to him. "Yeah. It's all in there."

"You think it's doable?"

"I'll have to look over the area, but I think so."

We drove out to Gunderson's office, and went slowly past it.

"I think it will work," Vince said.

"It's starting to get dark. Let's wait a few minutes," I said.

We drove down the road, parked, and waited about a half hour until the sun had disappeared.

"Now?" I asked.

Vince nodded. "Let's go."

"Watch for their security patrols, Vince "They come by every so often". Sure enough one came by a couple of minutes later.

"We should be all right for twenty minutes or so," I said.

"That ought to do it", he replied, "and if not, it's getting pretty dark out. Drive on down the road and come back for me in twenty minutes, OK?" He headed for the fence, carrying a small bag with him.

I returned in exactly twenty minutes, and Vince was waiting for me on the side of the road. He quickly jumped in the car and threw the small bag in the back seat.

"I think we're OK." he said, lifting his right thumb up in the air.

"Gunderson's car is still in the parking lot. I think we need to drop in on him."

"Let's do it," Vince replied.

I pulled into the parking lot. There were only a few cars left.

"I'd feel better if we had a little back up." I said.

Vince grinned. "We do."

He pointed at a car about thirty feet away. "A couple of the guys are in there."

As we got out of our car, two men emerged from that car. I recognized them immediately.

"Hey. That looks like Bill Butler and Fred Grogan."

"You got it." Vince replied.

"I'll be darned. How did you arrange that?"

"Well, they both live in Southern California now, and I figured they could use some action. They're probably both getting a little stale."

"Not those two," I replied. I had served with both of them, and they were top notch.

I went over and shook hands with both of them.

"Hey, guys. Great to see you! Wish the occasion was a little happier."

Bill nodded. "So do I. I understand some bad-ass is holding your wife, Brian."

"Yeah, I think so. I'm at least ninety-nine percent sure."

"That's good enough for me," Fred said. "What's the plan?"

"We're going in and talk to this man, and we'll play it by ear. He has an assistant named Moretti. I sure hope he's around. He's the guy who abducted Jenny."

Bill shook his head. "We will certainly look forward to meeting him."

I nodded. "I'm sure. Let's go in before Gunderson leaves."

"Is that the guy who runs all of this?"

"That's right."

"We will look forward to meeting him too."

"You guys packing?" Vince asked.

They both nodded. "Oh yeah." Fred replied.

"Let's go." I said.

We headed over to the guard-house.

The man inside looked us over curiously.

"Can I help you?"

"We're here to see Mr. Gunderson."

"Do you have an appointment?"

"No. Just tell him Brian McCarthy's here to see him."

He came back a couple of minutes later.

"Mr. Gunderson will see you. Someone will be over to escort you to his office. In the meantime I would like to search you."

"For what?" I asked.

"For anything that shouldn't go in the building."

"That won't really be necessary. But if it will make you feel better you can search me." I said.

"I need to search all of you."

"I'm afraid that won't be possible. My friends are very sensitive about things like that."

"Then they can't go in."

"You'd better check with Mr. Gunderson about that, because I'm not going in unless they do. Unsearched."

He left again, and returned looking unhappy.

"I guess that will be all right."

Another man, looking similar to Moretti showed up at the guard-house.

"Follow me" he said and started back toward the main building. When we got there he went over to the receptionist's desk.

I pointed to a group of chair over on the side.

"Let's sit over there, fellas."

Gunderson's secretary came over to them a few minutes later. "Mr. Gunderson will see you now."

I stood up. "Tell Mr. Gunderson that we will meet with him here in the lobby,"

"Mr. Gunderson would prefer to meet with you in his office."

"Tell Mr. Gunderson that we came all the way out here to see him, and we would prefer to meet with him right here. Otherwise we can leave."

"I will tell him." She walked away.

Bill Butler looked at me with a puzzled expression on his face. "Why this?" he asked.

I grinned at him. "Just wait and see, Bill."

Gunderson arrived a few minutes later.

"You are being very difficult, Mr. McCarthy."

"Where's my wife, Mr. Gunderson?"

"Your wife? I have no idea."

"Really? Well, there was a witness to the kidnapping. The perpetrator was identified as your Mr. Moretti."

"It sounds like you have a problem, Mr. McCarthy."

"Perhaps. You have quite a security set up, here. I see guards constantly patrolling the grounds."

"Yes. We are quite proud of it."

"I'm sure. Well, I want my wife back, Mr. Gunderson, and I want her back tonight. Now."

"I understand your concern, Mr. McCarthy. Perhaps if you and I had a better business relationship I might be able to do something to help you." He smiled, but it was a ugly, evil smile.

"Perhaps you're not aware of it, but my wife is two months pregnant.

"Really? That's interesting. I can see why you would be concerned."

"I want her back at my office by seven o'clock this evening. If she is not back, or has been harmed in any way, I will hold you personally responsible."

At this point Moretti walked into the lobby.

"You son of a bitch," I yelled at him. "Where is my wife?"

"You'll have to talk to someone else about that."

He was standing about two feet from me now, and I couldn't help myself. I swung a quick right at him, catching him up the gut. He doubled up, and then quickly straightened up, clutching a mean-looking knife in his right hand.

Before he could make a move, Bill Butler was pointing a jet black .45 at him.

"Your next move may be your last, fella," he said.

Moretti glared at me. "You're gonna pay for that," he said.

"Hold on everybody," I said. "Mr. Gunderson, I want you to sit right here." I pointed at a chair facing the front of the building and waited until he sat in it.

"We were talking before about your security system here at headquarters."

"That's right." he replied.

"You think it's pretty good?"

"It's very good."

"Well, I want to give you a demonstration of just how good it is."

"What do you mean?"

I took a small electronic pointer out of my pocket that Vince had given me earlier.

I pointed at the statue of his father outside the front of the building.

"That statue is of your father, I believe?"

"That is correct."

I pressed a button on the device, and there was a small explosion at the base of the statue, followed by a large puff of white smoke. Then the statue started slowly toppling backward toward the building. The head of the statue barely reached the glass window and smashed into it, shattering the glass, pieces of which flew all over the lobby. The cold air from outside suddenly blew through the reception area. The look on Hugo Gunderson's face was sheer astonishment.

"What have you done?" he demanded.

"That's nothing compared to what we'll do if my wife is not returned by seven o'clock." I glanced at my watch. "You have an hour and a half to return her to me. At my office. Unharmed."

Gunderson sneered at me. "Go to Hell, McCarthy."

"Wrong statement." I said, and slapped him hard in the face.

He started to get up out of the chair, but I pushed him back down.

"For your information, Mr. Gunderson, my wife Jennie is two months pregnant. If she has been mistreated or harmed in any way, you are a dead man walking. Do you understand?"

I doubt if anyone had ever talked to him this way, and he looked pretty shook up.

"Do you understand?" I said again. "Where is she now?"

"I don't know."

"Wrong answer." I slapped him again. "Where is she?" I raised my hand to hit him again. He blinked at me for a couple of seconds and covered his face.

"All right. She's at my house, and she's all right."

"OK. Let's go get her. Moretti you can go with us. I don't want you running around loose."

We all walked carefully over the broken glass and out the front door. I looked at Vince, "You got some hand cuffs in that bag of yours?"

"Yeah, sure."

"Good. Get me two pair, will you?"

Vince picked up the bag he had thrown in back seat of my car and fished two pairs of hand cuffs out of it.

"Let's cuff both of these character, hands behind their back. We'll put Gunderson in my back seat, and Moretti in Bill's car. Bill, follow us over. Gunderson, where do you live?"

"Bel Aire."

"That's about forty-five minutes from here. Let's go."

Chapter Twenty-Two

Bel Aire is a very high-end residential area North of downtown Los Angeles. It consists of winding roads, up and down hills with large homes, many of them gated mansions, on both sides of the street.

Gunderson's home was gated and he gave us the code to open it up. We drove in, parked the two cars and got out.

"Vince, take the cuffs off of Gunderson. I don't want his servants to be alarmed. Bill and Fred, you keep Moretti out here, and keep the cuffs on him. OK. Let's go.

The front door was unlocked and we went into a large entry area.

"All right, Gunderson. Where's my wife?" I had borrowed Bill's gun and waved it at him.

"Down the hall", he replied.

"Show me where."

We walked down the hallway, stopping in front of one doorway.

"In here," Gunderson said.

I opened the door, not knowing what to expect. What I saw was Jennie, tied to a chair, staring at us.

"Oh, Brian. I'm so glad to see you."

I walked over to the chair, gave her a quick kiss on her forehead and began untying the rope.

"We'll have you out of here in a minute, Babe. Are you all right?"

"Yes, I'm fine. At least now I am."

"You're sure you're all right? No one hurt you or bothered you? That looks like a bruise on your face. Where did that come from?"

"Oh, Moretti and I had a little tussle when I tried to knee him in the groin, but he didn't mean anything by it. It was sort of self defense." He had also fondled her breasts, but she didn't want to tell Brian that. She was afraid of what he might do to Moretti if he knew, and there wasn't really any harm done, just a little humiliation.

I turned to Gunderson. "We are going to leave now. We'll leave Moretti here."

"Good. I want you out of my house."

"Don't worry. And you can forget about Cavernite. We won't be doing any business. In fact I hope Belmont puts you out of business, you son-of-a-bitch."

"You'll pay for this, McCarthy. Nobody treats me this way."

"We'll see who pays for what. Let's get out of here, Vince."

We all got in our cars and returned to my office.

"What do you think?" Vince asked.

"I think that shook him up a little. By the way, Vince. Nice job. No body handles explosives the way you do."

"Hell, Brian. That was easy."

We all sat down around our small conference table and went over the events of the day.

"You sure you're all right, Jennie?"

"I'm fine, but God I was glad to see you. They just locked me in that room in Gunderson's house, but nobody touched me." She was home now and all right so she didn't see any point in getting Brian all stirred up. Besides, she'd had her breasts fondled before.

"Thank God. I don't feel like murdering anyone today."

I introduced her to Bill and Fred. "These are a couple of old Service buddies, and very handy to have around. Well, guys, I guess the party's over. I really appreciate your help."

Vince was shaking his head. "I'm not sure that you've heard the last of those two characters, Brian."

"Hey, listen, I appreciate your help. I couldn't have done it without you."

They both stood up. "Our pleasure, Brian," Bill said. "But if you have any more trouble with those guys, call us."

"I will." We shook hands and they walked out with Vince. "Talk to you soon, Vince. Where are you staying?"

"With Bill." I watched as the three of them left. What great guys!

I took Jennie in my arms. "God, it's good to see you, but you look a little tired."

"Yeah. I guess I didn't get a whole lot of sleep last night."

The next day we got together with the people from Belmont and signed all the necessary documents to turn the medication over to them.

They would build a small facility near the cave entrance to handle and process the Cavernite or whatever they decided to call it. I had told them about at the little scene out at the Koldex plant.

"I don't imagine Gunderson is expecting any further conversation with you."

"If I never see that man again that will be too soon. Well, I guess the security for the cave is your responsibility now."

"That's right," Harrison said. "We expect to send someone down there later this week to look it over. Do you think your man down there will be available?"

"Just let me know who's going down and when he will be there, and I'll arrange to have Jim meet him at the farm house. Anyway, I'm looking forward to our association, Jim"

"So am I. We'll have to get our PR people on this. How much publicity do you want on this, Brian? Personally, that is."

"Frankly, as little as possible, preferably none."

"All right, that can be arranged."

"One other thing, Jim. It seemed that Gunderson pretty much knew what was going on between us and your company. Too much. Somewhere there had to be a leak."

"Do you think it was at our end?"

"I have no idea, but I'm sure it wasn't at our end. The only two people that knew what was going on besides me were Jennie and Paul, and I would trust both of them with my life."

"Well, the only two people who knew about at Belmont were my Vice President, who'se been with me for twenty years, and my secretary Marla O'Conner. She's fairly new but I think I trust her."

"Well, the last time Gunderson called me he apparently knew that we can reached an agreement with you. He was angry, Jim and he threatened me. I'm not too worried about that. I can take care of myself, but I am concerned about Jennie. Gunderson comes across as a very nasty character."

"Look, I'll check at my end here and I'll get back to you."

"I would appreciate it."

He called me back about two hours later.

"Brian, I have to apologize. The leak was here. Marla admitted it when I confronted her. Apparently Gunderson offered her some money to keep him informed, and I guess she needed the money for an illness in her family."

"I'm sorry to hear that, Jim, for your sake."

"At least I found out, and Marla doesn't work here any more. I felt sorry for her in a way, but it's over, and I told her we would not prosecute. But she did need the money, and I wish she had come to me."

"At least you know."

"Yeah, I guess so, but it was very unpleasant and unsettling."

"Well, let's stay in touch, Jim. I'm anxious to get things going."

"So are we, Brian."

Back at Gunderson's house, he and Moretti were in deep conversation.

Gunderson was angry and humiliated. No one had ever treated him the way Brian McCarthy had. He was just furious.

"Those people are going to pay for that, Moretti."

"What do you want to do, boss?"

"It is clear that I will not be able to make a deal with him on that substance he discovered. It is also clear that it will do a great deal of harm to my company."

"So?"

"So we will have to destroy it. Here is what I want you to do. First of all, find someone who can take us down in the cave."

"Us?"

"Yes, us. I am going down in there with you."

"OK, if you say so."

"I do. The second thing I want you to do is get ahold of a flame-thrower. We're going to burn that room out."

"All right. Where do I get one?"

"I don't know. You have contacts, people who sell used military equipment, things like that. It shouldn't be very difficult."

Chapter Twenty-Three

It was close to three A.M. when the three men approached the cave entrance, moving slowly and silently.

One of them was carrying a metal saw. He looked at the metal gate across the entrance, and said "Give me a few minutes and I'll get us in there."

"Hurry up, Moretti," the big man said. "I don't want to take all night."

Moretti nodded. "Don't worry Mr. Gunderson. It won't take long." He began sawing on a part of the gate, and a few minutes later said created an opening that they could all get through, even the big man.

Once they were in, the third man, an experienced caver Moretti had hired for the night, ignited his head-lamp. He looked around for a minute and then pointed to his right. "It looks like it would be this way."

They started out in single file, the guide leading the way. Then the passage started to narrow. The big man found himself bending over more and more. He was also beginning to doubt the wisdom of this trip.

He had decided to go down in the cave in the first place because he was anxious to see just where this strange medication was growing, and wanted to make sure that it got destroyed. But now he wasn't sure it was a good idea at all. He was bothered by the inky blackness all around him, the feeling of isolation, and at times dizziness.

Moretti was also having a problem in the narrow passageway. He had the tank from the flamethrower strapped on his back.

Gunderson also knew that, up ahead of him, was that area of narrow ledge with the big drop-off. Moretti had told him about it, and he definitely wasn't looking forward to that. He thought about turning back but didn't want to expose his fears in front of Moretti, who had a big mouth.

They kept on moving ahead until the guide stopped.

"Looks like the path is getting narrower, and that looks like quite a drop-off on the left."

He took a flashlight out of his bag and pointed it over the side.

"Boy. Can't even see the bottom. Well, let's keep going, but be careful."

They began inching their way along the ledge, and Gunderson found himself becoming more and more nervous.

He finally spoke up.

"Maybe we ought to go back."

The guide responded, "Can't be too much further."

"How do you know?"

"That's usually the way these kinds of things are. We'll be OK."

"Yeah, but we have to come back out this way too, don't we?"

"Yes sir. We do."

Gunderson noticed now that the ledge was wet, and was becoming slippery. He found himself becoming more and more concerned.

"I don't know about this."

"Hang in there Mr. Gunderson. We'll be through this shortly."

Gunderson felt his foot slip on the ledge and became panicky, plus his dizziness had returned. He turned his body to face the wall and began grasping at it for a hand-hold, but the surface was smooth, solid rock, and there was nothing to grab ahold of. He began to sway back and forth, becoming desperate, grabbing at anything.

Moretti was now standing next to him, and he grabbed ahold of his arm.

Moretti yelled at him. "Let go, boss. You're going to kill both of us!"

He tried pushing his boss away from him, but Gunderson felt himself slipping away and held on to Moretti tighter as he toppled over the edge, falling into the blackness below, taking Moretti with him.

The guide said later that he could hear them both screaming all the way down as they fell into the darkness below, and then there were two thuds and silence.

The guide also told people that for a few nights after that, when he was home alone, and he woke up in the dark, he could still hear them screaming. "That was the end of cavin for me."

It was also the end of Koldex, which was hit with a double blow. First it lost its President, and then Belmont introduced it's new "miracle" cure for the cold. Koldex ended up closing its doors. The statue of it's founder remained lying on the ground in front of the empty, deserted building as mute testimony to it's demise.

When I heard the news about Gunderson and Moretti I must admit that I wasn't particularly upset. In fact, I was somewhat relieved that I wouldn't have to worry about them anymore, especially on Jennie's account.

Of course the cave received a great deal of notoriety because of the two death that had occurred there. Hundreds of people wanted to tour it, and we had to provide complete security for the foot traffic where the accident had occurred. At ten dollars a head it brought in a lot of income for several weeks, and continued nicely after that.

Meanwhile things were going great with Jennie and I. She had her baby, which of course was a girl. Mary McCarthy. The checks were starting to come in regularly from Belmont, and I had pretty much lost what little interest I had in the advertising business, so I sold the agency to the employees for a very reasonable price. Some of them had the cash and from others I took notes. I really wanted them to own it, and the last I checked on it, the enterprise was doing well.

With a lot of time on my hands, I decided to write a book about our adventures in the cave. I hope you enjoyed it.